BREAKING FREE

DELTA FORCE STRONG BOOK #4

ELLE JAMES

TWISTED PAGE INC

BREAKING FREE

DELTA FORCE STRONG BOOK #4

New York Times & *USA Today*
Bestselling Author

ELLE JAMES

Dedicated to my children who share my love of travel and adventure.
Elle James

AUTHOR'S NOTE

Enjoy other military books by Elle James

Ivy's Delta (Delta Force 3 Crossover)
Breaking Silence (#1)
Breaking Rules (#2)
Breaking Away (#3)
Breaking Free (#4)
Breaking Hearts (#5) coming soon
Breaking Point (#6) coming soon

Visit ellejames.com for titles and release dates
For hot cowboys, visit her alter ego Myla Jackson at
mylajackson.com
and join Elle James's Newsletter at
https://ellejames.com/contact/

CHAPTER 1

"I STILL DON'T UNDERSTAND why I got stuck with the job," Bull said.

Rucker pounded him on the back. "It's because you're the biggest, best looking guy on the team. Most of all, you know what manners are. The rest of us are clueless."

"I should never have told any of you that my mother sent me to a cotillion," Bull muttered.

"Got that right," Dash said. "That just opens you up to a whole lot of grief."

"Here, let me take a look at you." Blade stood in front of Bull and adjusted his collar. "I don't understand why they're not sending *me* in."

"Are you kidding?" Mac shook his head. "You think you're some kind of ladies' man. You'd be screwing every female in there."

"I'm not some horndog looking for a little tail." Blade grinned. "I'm a little more selective than that."

Rucker laughed. "Not much. Still...while Bull's eating steak and drinking wine with the hot shots, we'll be stuck bunking with each other, eating MREs."

"Not necessarily," Dash said. "We have our cover, too. We're supposed to be a mix of contractors and tourists, so we'll get a chance to sample some of the local cuisine."

"Yeah," Blade said, "but it won't be steaks like they'll be having at the embassy."

Bull would rather have stayed with the other guys. Being the lone man on the inside wouldn't be as much fun. "What exactly is my job inside?"

"To keep us informed," Rucker said. "The ambassador will fill you in when you get inside. It's supposed to be super-secret, just between us and him."

Bull swallowed a groan. Great, he'd probably be babysitting the ambassador the entire time. And he wouldn't be allowed to take in his M4A1 rifle. "Can I take *any* kind of weapon?"

"Maybe a pocketknife but *no* guns," Rucker said. "That's why we're sending in the biggest guy. You're the best one at hand-to-hand combat. You can take down just about anybody inside that compound. Hopefully, you won't have to though."

Blade grinned. "Look at you, all dressed up. You

almost look like a civilian." He stood in front of Bull, straightened the collar once more on the button-down dress shirt, adjusted the necktie and ran his gaze from top to toe. "Look pretty good to me. That cotillion practice did you some good."

Bull tugged at the knot at his neck. "I hate neckties."

"Consider it like you're taking one for the team," Dash said.

"Yeah, yeah," Bull muttered and glanced down at his watch. "Damn. I've only got fifteen minutes to get inside the compound to be on time for my meeting with the ambassador."

"Better get going," Rucker said. "You know where we'll be for the most part. You have your cellphone in case you need to get in touch with us, and a radio, should the cellphone get compromised."

Bull patted the pockets on his suit and grabbed the handle of his black, wheeled suitcase.

"Now, remember your name is Greg Smith," Rucker reminded him.

"Greg Smith," he repeated.

"You have everything?" Rucker asked.

Bull patted the fake passport in his pocket and glanced down at his suitcase. "I think so."

"The guard at the gate should let you in, no problem." Rucker stood back and looked him over. "Let's go through the checklist. Passport.

Bull patted his right pocket. "Check."

"Cellphone."

Bull dug in his left pocket. "Check."

"Radio headset in your ears now."

A hand to his ear confirmed Bull had the earbuds in place. "Check."

"Formal wear."

Bull touched the handle of his suitcase "Inside the suitcase. Check."

"Dress shoes?"

Again, he tapped the suitcase. "Also, inside the suitcase. Check."

"Condoms," Blade piped in with a grin.

Rucker back-handed Blade in the belly. "He's going in on a job, not to play."

"Never go anywhere without them." Blade crossed his arms over his chest. "If you're a good boy scout, you're always prepared."

Bull didn't mention that he'd been an Eagle Scout, nor did he mention that he did have condoms packed in his shaving kit. Only because they were already there. Not because he thought he'd need them.

Rucker clapped his hands together. "You're ready. The taxicab will pick you up in front of the hotel across the street in T-minus-two minutes. You'd better get on down there."

"I expect an extraction operation if things get terminally dull," Bull said.

"Ha," Rucker said. "I'm sure you'll find something interesting to keep you from being bored."

Dash chuckled. "You'll just have to deal with it and drink tea with your pinky sticking out."

"I don't drink tea," Bull growled.

"Well, you may have to suffer a little while you're inside. If you're entertaining Turks, they like their tea."

"I'd rather have a beer." Bull would give anything for one at that very moment. He'd chug it for that little bit of buzz it would give him. It might take the edge off.

"You'll have to draw on your cotillion experience," Rucker said. "That's why you're the chosen one."

"Thanks, Mom," Bull muttered beneath his breath. He tugged once more at the tie around his neck and nodded. "I'm ready."

"Break a leg, cowboy," Dash called out.

Rucker clapped him on the back. "Remember to report in once you've settled in and gotten your assignment."

"Roger." Bull left the hotel through a side entrance, circled the block, crossed the street and came back to the hotel where the taxicab was waiting for him. He entered the side of the hotel and came out the front. The taxi was there, waiting, the driver standing by the rear door.

Bull handed him the address for the U.S Embassy, stashed the suitcase in the trunk and climbed into the backseat of the taxi. The embassy was barely a block away and within sight of the hotel where his buddies would be *roughing* it.

In the blink of an eye, the taxi pulled in front of the U.S. Embassy.

"I'll walk from here." He paid the driver and got out of the cab. At the gate, he presented his passport. The guard checked it thoroughly, had him load his suitcase into an x-ray scanner and directed him to walk through the body scanner. The scanner went off and the guard made him back out.

"Sir, please place your cellphone, keys and anything else in the tray, and then go back through."

He emptied his pockets into a tray then walked back through the scanner. He worried that the radio headset might set it off, but he went through without a warning beep.

"Sir, please follow me." One of the guards led him to the embassy building and left him at the front reception desk.

"May I help you, sir?" A woman dressed in a conservative navy skirt suit glanced up over the top of her glasses. "Do you have an appointment?"

Bull nodded. "I do. With Ambassador Grey."

"One moment, sir." She checked his passport, nodded, and then hit the button on the phone in front of her. A couple minutes later, a man in a business suit emerged from an elevator and strode across to the reception desk.

"Mr. Smith, if you'll come with me, I'll take you to the ambassador."

He followed the man into the elevator, and it rose to the top floor. They exited and walked down a hallway to an office. A middle-aged secretary with brown hair and wire-rimmed glasses manned the desk outside the office. She glanced up with a welcoming smile. "Good afternoon, Mr. Smith."

His escort stepped back, turned and walked away.

"You can leave your suitcase here." The secretary pointed to the side of her desk then motioned toward a door. "Ambassador Grey will see you right away."

He parked the suitcase next to her desk and walked through the door. A tall man with graying hair stood up from behind his desk and crossed the room with his hand held out. "Mr. Smith, so glad you could come."

He took the man's hand in a firm grip. "Nice to meet you, Ambassador Grey."

"Please, have a seat." The ambassador motioned toward a conference table in the corner of the room. He went back to his desk and punched a button on his phone. "Ms. Moore, could you call her one more time? Thank you." He shook his head as he walked across to the conference table and sat in the chair at the end. "I appreciate you and your team getting here so fast."

"Yes, sir. What exactly do you want us to do while we're here?"

"As you know, the government in Turkey isn't as stable as it once was. The president has made it more of a military state than a democracy. There have been multiple uprisings, making it more and more dangerous for diplomats, their families and tourists. I'm concerned about my staff. I don't believe the security details assigned to the embassy are enough. They're doing a good job, but if the embassy were stormed, there's no way we would be able to fend off a large-scale attack."

"Sir, the addition of my team might not be enough either."

The ambassador nodded. "I understand that. What I want from your team on the outside is an early warning. And anything they can do to slow down an attack or get my people out before such an assault."

Bull nodded. That was the briefing the Delta Force team had been given.

"As for you," the older man drew in a deep breath and let it out. "I have an entirely different assignment."

Bull's brow furrowed. "Sir?"

The door to the ambassador's office burst open, and a dark-haired young woman rushed in. "Sorry, ambassador," she said as she hurried across to sit in one of the chairs at the conference table. "I had the driver make a detour on my way back from the elementary school. We stopped at the shopping mall so that I could pick up a gift for Ms. Moore's birthday." Once she'd settled in her seat, she glanced across at Bull and then back at the ambassador. "What's this meeting all about?"

The ambassador turned to Bull. "Layla, this is Greg Smith. Mr. Smith, my daughter Layla. She will be your assignment."

Layla glanced from Bull back to the ambassador. "Wait...what?"

Bull blinked. "Sir?"

"That's right, Mr. Smith. Your job inside the embassy is to gather intel wherever you can, but your number one priority will be looking after the safety and security of my daughter, Layla."

"But, Daddy," Layla said, "I don't need a bodyguard. I already have a couple of guards who follow me around."

"And you keep losing them," the ambassador said with a frown.

Her dark eyebrows swooped downward. "I can't help it they can't keep up with me."

"Your previous guards couldn't go with you everywhere," her father said, "and that's how you were getting away from them."

"I wasn't intentionally trying to lose them," Layla said.

Her father gave her a tight-lipped glare. "Things are getting a little bit too volatile around here for you to be out on the streets by yourself."

Layla leaned back in her seat. "What about sergeants Mitchell and Ramirez? Are you firing them?"

The ambassador shook his head. "They'll still be assigned as your escorts when you leave the embassy compound."

Layla's frown deepened. "You're telling me that I'm to have *three* bodyguards now as I leave the embassy compound? Do you know how hard it is to get three people into a cab? Now I'm going have to get four into a cab?"

"You'll have to make do. And as part of his intelligence gathering function, Mr. Smith will be by your side at every event—dinners, socials and balls."

"How am I supposed to perform my social functions when I have a bodyguard standing next to me?"

"I've thought about that." Her father smiled. "We will present Mr. Smith as your fiancé, not your bodyguard. Your fiancé will be invited to all the functions and all the gatherings, without question. He'll sit at the table with you, stand beside you in receiving lines and basically be your shadow everywhere you go."

Layla rolled her eyes and groaned. "Seriously, Daddy? I'm a grown woman. I don't need a babysitter. Haven't I functioned as your hostess without fail?"

He nodded and laid his hand across his daughter's. "I'm not questioning your ability. I'm just concerned about your safety."

"Daddy, I don't need another bodyguard."

His lips firmed. "The decision has been made. If you are to stay here at the embassy, you will accept Mr. Smith's protection without question. If you can't do that, then I need to put you on the next plane home."

Layla leaned toward her father. "Daddy, you need me here."

"I don't need you here if it means risking your life." His brow dipped, and his voice deepened. "If the situation gets any hotter, I *will* send you home."

She snorted. "Home? And where might that be? You sold the house I grew up in. We don't have a home back in the United States."

"Home *is* the United States," he said.

"I have more family here in Turkey than I do back in the US."

"Your mother's relatives don't recognize you as part of their family. They disowned her when she married me. What makes you think that they would accept you in their homes?"

Layla frowned. "I'm working on that."

"You do that," the ambassador said, "as long as you take Mr. Smith with you and stay off the streets when the riots start." He looked from Bull to Layla and back to Bull. "I suggest the two of you come up with a cover story for your engagement." He fished a small square box out of his pocket and handed it to Bull. "This was Layla's mother's engagement ring. I

11

had it sized to fit Layla's finger. As of this moment, the two of you are officially engaged."

Bull's gut knotted. "Sir, I'm not sure I want to be a part of this. I'm a soldier, not an actor."

The ambassador chuckled. "Trust me, Mr. Smith, you're going to need every bit of your army training, especially your Delta Force skills, to stay up with my daughter. And to keep her safe."

The ambassador pushed back from the table. "The people in this room are the only three people who will know that this engagement isn't real. That it's a cover. You're not to share that information with anybody else, except maybe your team, if they need to know. But they can't share that information with anyone else." He stared at his daughter. "And you'll make it look real. I've assigned Mr. Smith to the room beside yours, Layla. The closer he is to you the better he can accomplish the job of keeping you safe."

"But Daddy, the embassy is surrounded by guards."

He nodded. "And they're doing an admirable job," he agreed. "But we've seen what's happened in other countries where embassies are attacked. They can be quickly overwhelmed by numbers. I want to know that you're going to be safe. That the man in charge of your security can get you the heck out of here if the walls are breached."

Layla frowned. "Do you know something that you're not telling me?"

Her father's eyes narrowed. "You know the situation here. The government is run by a president who would make himself dictator. The people aren't happy. The military is keeping them from staging an uprising. I think it's only a matter of time before there's rioting in the streets. And as you well know, not everybody is pro-American. So, humor me," her father said. "Play along with this charade, at least until the political environment calms down a bit." He nodded toward Bull. "I'm counting on you to keep my daughter safe."

Bull nodded, his chest and gut tight. "Yes, sir."

"Now if you'll excuse me, I have a meeting to attend." The ambassador spun on his heel and walked out of the room.

Layla stared across the table at Bull. "I don't plan on slowing down so that you can keep up with me."

Bull nodded. "Understood." He opened the ring box and stared down at a beautiful black sapphire and diamond ring. "Keep in mind that it might be strange if people see you dodging your fiancé."

She snorted. "You're not my fiancé. We're not engaged."

"According to your father's script, we are." He shoved the ring box toward her. "Do you need a formal declaration of my commitment to protect you?"

"No," Layla said. "I most certainly do not."

"Look, it's not like I *want* to be engaged to you. You're not even my type."

She frowned. "And what's wrong with my type?"

"Nothing if a guy likes a spoiled little rich girl."

"Spoiled little…" She clamped her lips shut and glared at him. "Look, I'm not spoiled. I work hard for my father, and I'm not even paid for it. I do it because I love him, and he needs the support of somebody to perform the functions that a wife normally would."

"And what about your mother?" he asked.

Layla's gazed dropped to the ring box. "My mother died of cancer the year my father was assigned as ambassador to Turkey."

"I'm sorry to hear that," Bull said. He understood how cancer could ravage a person and the family. "What kind of cancer?"

"Pancreatic cancer," she said. "From diagnosis to death was only six weeks." She glanced up, her eyes glassy with unshed tears. "My dad went from her funeral to an airplane to fly to Turkey. I couldn't let him do it alone."

His chest tightened. He wasn't good with female tears. "What about your job?"

"My father's work became my job." She lifted the ring in the box. "She was a really good woman. She made my father very happy. Her family could never understand why she married him, and pretty much cut her off."

"Then why did your father accept a position of ambassador to the country she was raised in?"

"They both hoped that they could work things out with her family. But after my mother's death, my father wasn't as willing to work with her family. He knew how much it broke her heart that they'd cut her off."

"I'm sorry about your mother. I lost my mother to cancer as well. She was far too young to leave this world."

Layla nodded. "Mine, too. She had a lot left to accomplish and never got around to it. She loved her husband, she loved her new country, but she loved her home as well."

Bull couldn't say that he was happy about his assignment, but it was his assignment and he needed to execute it. "Look," he said, "like it or not, we're stuck with each other. We need a cover story, and you need to put this ring on your finger. Where would you like to say we met?"

"I don't care. Pick a spot."

"It has to be some place that you've actually been."

"And you," she said. "Have you ever been to New York City?"

He shook his head.

"How about Miami, Florida?"

Again, he shook his head.

She cocked a single eyebrow. "San Diego?"

He shook his head.

"I went to school at Yale. Any chance you're familiar with Yale?" she asked.

"No," he said.

"Well, where have you been?"

"I grew up near San Antonio, Texas. Have you been there?"

She shook her head. "Good grief, there has to be at least one place that we've both been. What about high school? Where'd you go to high school?"

"In Texas."

"Vacation?"

"Cancun, Mexico?" he suggested.

She shook her head.

"Myrtle Beach, South Carolina?"

Her eyes widened. "I've been there."

"Okay, we've picked a place where we met. We met at Myrtle Beach, South Carolina."

"That was painful," Layla said. "At this rate, we won't have a full backstory until sometime next year. Like when did you propose?"

"I came here to ask your father for your hand in marriage, and then turned around and proposed to you." He took the ring box, got down on one knee and held it out in front of her. "Layla Grey, would you do me the honor of becoming my fiancée for the duration of this assignment?"

Her lips twitched, and the light danced in her eyes. When her lips spread into a smile, the look on her face hit Bull square in the chest.

She held out her ring hand. "Why, Mr. Smith, because my father told me I had to, I accept your offer for the duration of your assignment."

He took the ring from the box and slid it on her ring finger. "I guess then it's official. We got engaged here in your father's office, because you couldn't stand to be apart from me any longer. Ever since we met at Myrtle Beach, South Carolina. How long ago?"

"A year and a half," she answered. "It was our last vacation with my mother."

He nodded. "I could have been there."

"Good, now that that's done..." She pushed to her feet. "I need to get ready for dinner."

He fell in step beside her as she headed for the door. "Since you know where your room is, and my room is next to yours, I'll follow you."

Layla frowned, stopped and faced him. "Just because we're engaged, doesn't mean that you get to take any liberties."

He smiled. "And what kind of liberties would those be?"

Her brow formed a V over her nose. "You know what I'm talking about."

"I don't know," he said, a smile fighting to be free on his lips. "I'm just a dumb soldier. Maybe you'd better spell it out for me."

Her eyes narrowed. "Suffice it to say...hands off."

He held up his hands. "I told you, you're not my type. I usually go for blondes."

She touched a hand to her dark hair. "Well, that should make it easier then."

He nodded. "I'm not at all interested in you, so you don't have to worry." He cocked a brow. "Don't forget though, we're a newly engaged couple. We have to make everything look real."

"How so?" she asked.

He straightened, towering over her. "I would assume a newly engaged couple would at least hold hands."

Her brow puckered. She thought about it. "I guess that'll be all right."

He moved closer. "A newly engaged man would put his arm around his fiancée like this." He placed his hand at the small of her back.

"Don't push it, soldier," she warned.

His hand fell to his side. "We'll work on that."

"When we're alone," she said, "there's no need for us to pretend. We can be ourselves."

He nodded. "But when we're in company, we'll have to show a little bit of that PDA."

"PDA?" she asked, her dark eyebrow arching delicately.

"Public display of affection," he clarified.

"I don't know about that," she said.

He held out his hands. "You want people to buy into this charade, don't you?"

"Not really," she replied. "It's my father's idea."

"You don't want to disrespect your father, do you?" Bull asked.

Layla sighed. "No. I don't. But I don't want you hovering over me."

"I promise not to hover," he said.

"Good, now I've really got to get going. My father has strict rules about being at dinner on time. Sometimes, we have guests, and he doesn't like to keep them waiting."

"Very well." He waved a hand toward the door. "Lead the way."

Bull had to hurry to keep up with her. He snagged his suitcase as he passed the secretary's desk, and they walked on to the elevator. They descended a floor, got out and walked down a long corridor.

"I have the last room on the end. Apparently, yours is beside mine. When I go to bed at night, I don't like to be disturbed. I don't get up in the morning until at least eight o'clock, and I don't like people to talk to me until I've had my first cup of coffee."

He tapped his heels together and popped a salute. "Yes, ma'am."

Her brow descended. "And I don't like when people patronize me."

He grinned. "Yes, ma'am."

"And you can't go around calling me ma'am if we're supposed to be engaged."

"Yes—" He paused. "What do you want me to call you? Do I have a pet name for you?"

She shook her head. "I've never had a pet name or nickname."

"Well, your given name is Layla. I could call you Layla or my pet name for you could be Lolli."

She rolled her eyes. "No, just no. Call me Layla. And I can't call you Mr. Smith."

He'd be hard pressed to answer to it anyway, since his last name wasn't Smith. "Well, my first name is Greg," he said. It was Craig, but she didn't need to know that. He was undercover, and it was close enough. Craig sounded enough like Greg, that he wouldn't get confused. "My friends call me Bull."

Layla frowned. "Don't your friends like you?"

He laughed. They called him Bull because his real last name was Bullington. For the duration of the assignment, his last name was Smith. He couldn't tell her about the true nature of his nickname being a derivative of his real last name. Instead, he waved a hand in front of him. "I'm so large, my friends call me Bull because they think I'm like a bull in a china shop.

She nodded with a smile. "I can see that."

"You can call me Greg, or you can call me Bull. I don't care."

She stared at him for a long moment. "I think I'll call you Bull. But not because of a bull in a china shop, but more because of the bullshit we're having to put up with." She grinned. "Yeah, I like it. I'm gonna call you Bull."

It didn't bother Bull. His friends had called him worse.

She walked toward her room. "I leave for dinner at fifteen minutes before the hour. If you plan to escort me down, be ready."

He nodded. "What's the uniform for the evening?"

She shook her head. "We have to work on that military speak. Dinner attire is formal. You'll need a black suit and tie."

Thank goodness he'd packed one. Now all he needed was an iron to get out all of the wrinkles.

Layla ducked into her room.

He entered his, tossed his suitcase up on the bed and rummaged through it to find the suit they'd come up with for the assignment. Thankfully they'd found one off the rack in a store downtown.

It wasn't a perfect fit, but it was close enough. The entire time he was getting ready, he listened for the sound of her door opening. If he was to keep her safe, he needed to be with her twenty-four-seven. Being one door away from her, was one door too many. But Bull was absolutely certain she would not agree to him sleeping in the same room as her. He'd have to make do and keep his ears open.

Fifteen minutes before the hour, he stepped out into the hallway.

Layla's door opened, and she emerged wearing a

long black dress that hugged her from her breasts to her thighs and fell down in soft folds to her ankles. On her feet, she wore high heeled, strappy sandals sprinkled with shiny crystals. She'd swept her glorious dark hair up into a sleek arrangement at the back of her head with tiny tendrils of hair drifting down along her neck. Sparkly diamond hoops dangled from her ears, and a matching pendant nestled above her cleavage, held in place with a gold chain.

Bull's breath caught in his throat.

The woman was stunning. Dark, sultry and so beautiful, he could barely draw in a deep breath.

Her gaze raked over him, and she nodded with a small smile. "Not bad, for a soldier."

Bull silently thanked his mother for forcing him to train for and attend cotillion. He'd recognize the place settings and the numerous eating utensils beside the plates. At least, he wouldn't have to guess which one to use for what. He could practically guarantee that none of the other men on his team would know a salad fork from a prawn fork.

But his dinner partner...

Wow.

Bull prayed he didn't trip over his new dress shoes as he escorted her down the hallway to the elevator.

CHAPTER 2

LAYLA HAD SIGHED as she'd stepped out of her assigned quarters, fully expecting to see a soldier trying to dress up like a gentleman and wondering how he would behave in front of all the dignitaries that usually sat with them at dinner.

He probably wouldn't know one fork from another in the place settings. It was enough of an effort for her to play hostess without her trying to keep an eye on her dinner partner to make sure he didn't commit some faux pas that would insult their guests.

As she'd turned to close her door, she'd spotted Bull standing in the hallway. Her breath had caught. For a moment she'd stood still, drinking in the tall, gorgeous drink of water that was her fake fiancé. The old saying of *a suit maketh a man* could easily be turned around to say this man made that suit.

Most tall, broad-shouldered men looked bulky in formal attire. Not this guy. He wore the suit like a second skin, his shoulders filling the jacket to perfection. His trousers accentuated his long legs, making him appear even taller.

He'd given her a tight smile. "You look lovely, my dear," he said and held out his hand.

"There's nobody around right now," she whispered. "You don't have to pretend to be my fiancé."

He continued to smile, his hand still held out in front of him. In a low tone only she could hear, he said. "There's a camera in the corner that I'm certain takes in all of this hallway. Smile and come give me a kiss."

As irritated as she was, she took his hand and let him pull her into his arms.

"That's more like it," he said.

"Don't push it," she whispered, and leaned up to brush his lips with hers. The spark of electricity that passed between them left her lips tingling.

Yes, she knew there were cameras in the hallway, but she'd forgotten that she needed to put on a show for anyone and everyone who might be watching. She should be glad that he had remembered. Instead, she was irritated and now strangely aware of how soft his lips were against hers. Which irritated her even more.

The last thing she needed was to get involved with a bodyguard. Not that she had plans to get involved with Bull. He was just one more person who stood in the way of getting her work done. One more person she'd have to dodge later on this evening. She had no doubt that she could though. She'd gotten around every other bodyguard assigned to her, her personal assistant and her father.

She didn't do it out of spite or because she was a spoiled little rich girl. She did it out of need. A need to help others less fortunate than her, but that was a concern for later that evening. Right now, she had to get through a boring dinner, playing host with her father, since her mother wasn't there to perform the function of hostess to her father's host. It was up to her to support her father in his important duties as the US ambassador to Turkey. He was their country's number one representative in a country that was struggling beneath a president who would be a totalitarian if he had his way.

Bull took her hand, looped it through his elbow and patted her arm. "Ready?"

She had been a moment ago, but now she was just a little bit unsure. This man was not like her other bodyguards. His movements were like that of a dancer, clean and smooth, and his bearing was one of a gentleman.

She glanced up at him. "What branch of the service did you say you were in?"

His lips twitched as he whispered, "Army."

"Officer or enlisted?"

A smile spread across his face. "Enlisted."

"What are they teaching in basic training nowadays?" she asked.

He stared straight ahead. "How to carry a gun and shoot people."

Layla walked beside him to the elevator. So, he knew how to address a woman and to walk with her, but would he know how to sit at a dinner table and carry on a decent conversation, without saying something that could start a war?

"Do me a favor tonight," she said.

"Yes, ma'am."

"Don't speak unless you're spoken to. And only answer questions yes or no. The less you say, the better. Unless you're asked how we met, then you can tell them our story."

His lip curled up on one side. "Anything else?"

She shot him a narrow-eyed glance, looking for sarcasm in his expression.

His face was poker straight.

"Yes, don't call me ma'am. It makes me feel old." She smiled and sailed through the open door of the elevator, pulling him in with her. Knowing the elevator also had a camera, she kept smiling all the way down to the floor with the formal dining room.

Her father met them at the elevator. "Layla, you look lovely." He kissed both of her cheeks and shook hands with Bull. "Good, good, you look wonderful, too," he said as he released Bull's hand. "This dinner will give us a good opportunity to announce my daughter's engagement."

Bull dipped his head in a nod.

"Are you ready?" he asked.

Layla glanced up at Bull, and he caught her gaze.

They nodded at the same time.

"Good." The ambassador turned toward the dining room. "Tonight's guest is the head of the Ministry of Justice."

"That should be interesting," Layla said, "considering the president has his own idea of justice. Or is it just the justice minister's turn to spy on the Americans?"

Her father ignored her comment and continued. "The minister's name is Murat Akar, and he's brought with him a friend, Hasan Saka. Hasan is a Turkish businessman who supplies the Turkish army with beans and bullets."

Layla's eyes narrowed. "Interesting that he's a friend of the Minister of Justice. Is it a case of they're in bed together? Or is it a case of keep your friends close and your enemies closer?"

"Whatever the case is," her father said, "I just want to get through the evening without stirring up anything. Turkish government officials are touchy lately."

She smiled and patted her father's arm. "We'll do our best."

He smiled and laid his hand over hers. "Thank

you. I don't know what I would do without you." He smiled across at Bull. "And that's why she has you."

Bull tipped his head in acknowledgement.

"Shall we?" the ambassador said. He held out his arm.

Layla took her father's elbow.

Bull fell in step behind them.

As they entered the dining room, Layla's assistant, Pinar Erim, approached her, carrying a clipboard. "I arranged the seating as requested, Ambassador Grey."

Layla glanced at her father.

He nodded. "I asked Ms. Erim to seat the Minister of Justice to my right and his guest to his right. You will be seated on my left, Layla, and your fiancé will be seated to your left." Her father led the way to where the Minister of Justice and his guest stood and began the introductions.

After introducing himself to his two guests the ambassador turned to his daughter. "And this is my daughter, Miss Layla Grey. And I am pleased to introduce to you her friend, Greg Smith."

The minister shook Layla's hand and then Greg's.

Hasan Saka took her hand next and stared into her eyes, his narrowing just slightly. "It is an honor." He held her hand just a couple seconds longer than was necessary.

If he'd held on longer, Layla would have jerked her hand free. Fortunately, he let go before she hit her boiling point.

Layla understood that she was in an area of the world that didn't value women as highly as men. She'd gotten used to biting her tongue and had found a way to fight back in an entirely different way.

Layla gritted her teeth and smiled. "It is a pleasure to meet you." She'd been to enough dinners to know how to be polite and keep her opinions to herself. She was there as a hostess, not a game changer.

They took their seats around the table, and dinner was served by an excellent waitstaff. Layla made it all the way through dinner without visibly yawning. By the time the dinner plates were being cleared, her cheeks hurt, and she was ready to run screaming from the room. She'd done her duty of speaking about weather and places she'd visited in Turkey.

Bull had sat beside her talking only when spoken to and using all the correct utensils, which astounded her.

As the waitstaff cleared the dinner plates and brought in the dessert, a raspberry sorbet, she leaned close to Bull. "Are they teaching table etiquette in basic training nowadays?" she whispered.

He shook his head. "Not hardly."

"So where did you learn yours?" she asked.

"You can thank my mother and cotillon."

Her eyes widened. She looked into his. "Seriously?"

He nodded. "Much to my teenage humiliation and dismay."

She chuckled. "I can just picture it."

At the end of the table, her father cleared his throat. "I'd like to make an announcement," he said. All the guests at the table turned to the ambassador. "I have my staff serving up champagne and sparkling water, to those who don't drink alcohol, for a toast. I have reason to celebrate this evening."

He turned to Layla. "My daughter had a visitor today." The ambassador nodded at Bull. "Mr. Greg Smith, for those who haven't yet been introduced." The ambassador lifted his chin, a smile lifting his lips. "Mr. Smith came to my office to ask for my daughter's hand in marriage."

A collective *oh* went up from the ladies at the table.

"After listening to his reasons and declaration of love, I've granted him my blessing for their union. He asked my daughter, she has agreed to be his bride, and I'm pleased to announce, my daughter is engaged to be married."

The guests at the table clapped and congratulated the ambassador, Layla and Bull.

The waitstaff set glasses of champagne beside each guest. The ambassador raised his glass. "To my daughter and her fiancé. Hear! Hear!"

Layla smiled and nodded her acknowledgement. Bull did the same. The stage was fully set. She was now the proud future bride to the handsome Mr. Smith. Now, all she had to worry about was how she was going to get out of the embassy that night. With not one...not two...but three bodyguards watching her every move. Thank goodness the embassy had some secret staircases built in for the possibility that the embassy staff would need to escape quickly. She had made use of those hidden doorways, corridors and underground exits. Her bodyguards were never the wiser, and her newest one wouldn't be either.

The Minister of Justice glanced across the table at her and Bull. "Congratulations, Ms. Grey and Mr. Smith. Marriage is a sacred undertaking. It is refreshing to see a modern woman embracing such an old tradition."

"Thank you, minister," Layla said with a gracious smile.

"Thank you, Minister Akar," Bull acknowledged with a nod.

The man beside the minister raised his champagne glass. "I, too, would like to congratulate you. It amuses me that, in a country where marriages are entered for love, the divorce rate is so very high."

Layla pressed her lips together. "I'd prefer not to comment on that."

"Please, Ms. Grey, I'd like to know your opinion."

She took a deep breath and exchanged glances with her father.

When he gave a nod, she spoke, "In my country we can choose to marry for love, and when one of the partners in that marriage violates the vow, my people can choose to end the marriage. A woman does not have to stay in a loveless marriage. My people have the choice of staying or leaving. They're not forced to enter or stay in a marriage not of their choosing."

Saka's eyes narrowed. "I would assume by your statement that you do not approve of arranged marriages, as they are not entered by choice or by love."

She dipped her head. "I do my best to respect other cultures."

"But you do not approve, do you?" Saka's thick eyebrow lifted.

"I prefer not to comment, sir."

Her father quickly changed the subject, and the meal ended. Not soon enough for Layla. When she could escape, she did and headed back toward her room with Bull by her side. As soon as they were out of earshot of the guests, she muttered beneath her breath, "I can't believe that man put me on the spot. That was rude, even by Turkish standards. I can't abide by men who bully women."

"You're in the wrong part of the world if you're expecting to see equality between men and women."

"I know." She sighed.

"Even though Turkey is more progressive than some of the other countries in the Middle East. It's still backwards in gender equality."

Once in the elevator, she turned to him. "Thank

you for being so polite and well-mannered at the table."

"I'm glad to know that I didn't embarrass you," he said.

"You'll have to thank your mother for me."

His lips formed a thin line. "I would, but she passed away five years ago."

"You're right. You told me that. Well, she'd be proud of you."

"I'd like to think so," he said. "She always encouraged me to follow my heart."

Layla's eyebrow rose. "And your heart led you to the army?"

He nodded. "I wanted to be a part of something bigger than myself. Something that I could do that would represent my country, and something that would make my mother proud."

"Well, you did all that. I thought you handled Saka quite well. I could tell that you were holding back. And I'm sure he could, too. It was like he was trying to get a rise out of me. What do you think about arranged marriages?" she asked.

"I don't believe in forcing anyone to marry anyone else. And I especially don't think that children should be forced into marriages."

Layla nodded. "You've fought in the Middle East. I'm sure you've seen things that you can't unsee and you can't change.

He nodded.

"What if you could change things?" she asked. "Would you?"

He nodded. "But one person can't change an entire culture."

"Maybe not," she said, "but one person might change the outcome for one other person. That's one life changed for the better."

He nodded. By that time, they were standing in front of the door to his assigned quarters.

"I won't need you for the rest of the night," she said. "I'm going to curl up with a book, and then go to sleep early."

He nodded. "If you plan to go out, please let me know. I'll be in the room next door."

When she turned to walk away, he snagged her arm. "That's not how a newly engaged couple parts." He pulled her into his arms and bent his head to capture her lips with his.

At first, she was stiff, surprised by his action, but as the kiss continued, her body melted into his, and she returned the pressure on his lips, opening to him. He thrust his tongue past her teeth and caressed hers in a long slow glide, crushing her closer to him until she didn't know where his body ended and hers began.

As suddenly as he'd started, he stepped back. "Goodnight, my love," he said, and winked.

She turned as if in a daze, walked down the corridor to her room, entered, and closed the door behind her. Once she clicked the lock in place, she leaned her back against the wood paneling and remembered to breathe.

Holy hell. Where had he learned to do that? Layla was certain it wasn't at cotillion, nor was it in Army Basic Combat Training.

What she wasn't prepared for, was her desire to do it again.

CHAPTER 3

BULL HAD SAT THERE during that dinner playing the dutiful fiancé, all the while fighting the urge to reach out and touch the silky black dress Layla wore. Her dark hair and sultry eyes had captivated him from the beginning. But seeing the outline of her body in that simple black dress had revved his engines and left him half hard all night long.

When they'd reached the corridor outside their rooms, he'd had to do something, and he'd had the perfect excuse. Kissing her had been as natural as breathing. The problem was that once he'd kissed her, he wanted to do it again. He had also wanted to follow her to her bedroom and take that kiss just a little bit farther. But that would make him no better than his buddy Blade who kissed every female he came in contact with, or so it seemed.

Bull was on a mission, not on a vacation. He shouldn't be taking advantage of the situation. Although, his kiss had had a point. If they were being watched, they needed to show some public displays of affection. At least, that's how he justified it.

He entered his room, closed the door and locked it behind him. Stripping out of the suit, he pulled on a pair of jeans and a T-shirt. It was about time he reported in to his team. Not that he had much to report other than he'd made contact. And boy had he. His team would give him hell if they knew that he'd been kissing the ambassador's daughter.

What they didn't know wouldn't hurt him. He could tell them that he was pretending to be the daughter's fiancé. Beyond that, they didn't need to know the rest.

He engaged his headset. "Bull to the barnyard. Bull to the barnyard."

"Barnyard here," Rucker's voice came over his headset.

"The bull's in the china shop."

Rucker chuckled. "Who made up this shit?"

Bull laughed. "I think you can blame Dash."

"Oh yeah, that's right," Rucker said. "How'd it go? Did you get your assignment?"

He entered the bathroom and turned on the shower for background noise in case the room was bugged. "I met my fiancée."

"Say again?" Rucker's voice sounded surprised.

"That's right, I met my fiancée. I'll be sticking to her like glue."

"Or like a bull with a cow in heat?" Blade's voice sounded in his ear.

"I wouldn't go that far." Bull shook his head, an image of Layla in her black dress making him hard all over again. Layla was anything but a cow. She was beautiful and sexy in an exotic way. Not that his teammates needed to know that at this point.

"Is fiancée code for something that I didn't know?" Rucker asked.

"No code. Just cover."

"Ah-ha, that makes your assignment a lot more interesting."

"Anything to report out there?" Bull asked.

"All's quiet," Rucker said. "A few rumblings toward the center of town, but nothing this direction. Need anything from us?"

Bull couldn't think of anything. "Not at this point."

"Keep us informed."

"Roger." He ended the communication and turned off the shower. At that exact moment, he heard a door in the hallway open and then close. He hurried to his door and cracked it open just a hair. Enough to see out into the corridor. What appeared to be a young man in baggy jeans and a hoodie walked past his door, his head down, his face obscured by the sides of the hoodie. As he passed Bull's door, a waft of perfume assailed Bull's nostrils. The same perfume Layla had been wearing that evening.

He watched as the young boy walked by. The sway of his hips gave him away. Bull almost threw open the door and demanded, *What the hell?* Because the young boy was not a boy at all, but Layla Grey, the ambassador's daughter. And she appeared to be sneaking out of her room. For what purpose, Bull didn't know, but he'd find out.

Rather than ask her, he decided to follow her. He jammed his feet into running shoes and waited until she reached the end of the corridor and turned. Then he hurried after her. She had passed the elevator and gone down to another corridor. He raced to the end and peered around that corner.

At first glance, he thought he'd missed her. But then he saw a shadow move against the wall in the corridor to the right. Where was she going? Again, he hurried down that corridor and peered again to the right. She pushed through a stairwell door. He ran to the end of the hall and caught the stairwell door before it closed all the way. Easing it open, he slipped through, and then softly let it close.

Layla's feet made no noise on the staircase. She must have been wearing tennis shoes or something soft-soled. He glanced over the railing. Two floors below, a slim hand slid across the railing. Her hand disappeared, and a door opened below.

As quietly as he could, Bull hurried down the steps to the floor he guessed she had gotten out on. He cracked open the door and peered down the hallway. Her hooded figure pushed through a door halfway down the corridor. He waited until she went inside before he entered the hallway. When he reached the door, he looked at the sign posted over it. *Library*. Had she come down to the library to get that book she wanted to read? And would she be angry when she found him following her?

It didn't matter. His job was to follow her, to be with her every minute of the day. He pushed through the door and entered the library ready to confront her. As he did, he heard what sounded like gears turning. There were several stacks of books in orderly rows like any library back in the States, only on a smaller scale. He peered down each stack until he got to the end. A bookshelf in the middle of the final wall had just swung back into its position as if it had been a door closing.

"What the hell?" he muttered. He went to the case and tried pushing it. It didn't budge. Did it have a secret lever that needed to be pulled in order to open the door?

He tried moving different books. They all came out easily, none of them connected to a lever. Secret doors usually had some kind of hidden lever that would open them. He just had to find it, and soon, otherwise he'd lose her.

He tried a light switch on the wall, but it just turned out the lights. He felt along the bottom of the shelves to see if there was a button anywhere. He didn't find one. Finally, he tried pulling on a wrought iron sconce on the wall, the bookshelf shimmied. Bingo.

He pulled the sconce a little harder, and the shelf swung open revealing a narrow corridor. A narrow *empty* corridor. Damn. She had to be way ahead of him by now.

Bull entered the secret passage. The bookshelf swung closed behind him, and the corridor lit up. He ran down the corridor trying the catch up to the ambassador's daughter.

At one point, the corridor came to a T intersection. To the left it climbed. To the right it descended. If the ambassador's daughter was trying to sneak out, she would be going down. If she was trying to get back to her room, she might go up, but then why did she not come down that path to begin with?

Bull followed his gut and took the descending stairs. Where would she be going at that time of night? And why did she feel the need to sneak out?

Eventually, the stairs came to an end. The air was cooler and a little damp, as if they were in some kind of basement. A door opened up into yet another tunnel. By the smell and feel of it, it was an underground chamber leading he didn't know where. But he kept going, hoping that he would eventually run into Layla.

As he followed along, he began to think that perhaps he'd chosen the wrong direction, but then he came to a door. He pushed through it and peered out into what appeared to be an empty street. Then a shadow moved at the corner, and he recognized the hooded boy with the tantalizing perfume, slipping around a building.

He pushed through the door then looked back briefly. The door all but disappeared. It looked more like a vine-covered stucco wall. Anybody passing by would never know there was a door behind the vines. He committed the location to memory and jogged after Layla.

Now, he understood why the ambassador wanted him to follow his daughter around. Did the ambassador even know that his daughter was sneaking around at night? He might have had some inclination to know that he needed to assign a Delta Force soldier to keep up with her. She obviously knew her way around the embassy as well as around the town. She moved quickly and with the assurance of somebody who knew where she was going.

Bull didn't have time to notify his team. Even if he did, he didn't know exactly where he was. Thankfully, he still had his cellphone on him and his fake passport. If he needed to, he could get back to the embassy on his own and get inside. If he couldn't open the hidden gate, he'd have a challenge explaining how he'd gotten out without passing through the guards' post.

However, his first goal was to catch up with Layla.

CHAPTER 4

Layla hurried through the streets, hoping she wasn't too late. She had received the call from Miriam Rogers saying that the transfer had been moved up an hour instead of taking place at midnight. While Miriam was working to find a safehouse and transportation out of the country, someone needed to get their subject out of her current situation before it was too late. With all of her contacts tied up in other efforts, Miriam had called Layla as a last resort.

Layla had known about the operation but had expected somebody else to handle it. She was supposed to have assisted at the safehouse where she was least likely to be exposed or captured.

She hadn't gone looking to get involved in this whole underground operation. It had more or less fallen in her lap when she'd moved to Turkey with her father. Had she not run into Miriam at a coffee shop, she would've gone through her father's entire assignment blissfully ignorant of what was going on in the city. But now that she knew, she couldn't just stand back and let it happen. Women were not cattle. They were not meant to be bought, sold and traded like animals. She had entered the scheme thinking that, if she could save only one woman, that was one woman who wouldn't have to go through the horror of being sold into the sex trade or sold into a marriage she had no desire to be in.

Not only had she helped save one woman, but she'd also helped to save more than a dozen. The women were spirited out of the country and found homes elsewhere in the world, where they could live out their lives as they pleased and not as somebody else forced them.

The coordinator of the effort was Miriam Rogers, who had a network of women spread throughout the city and beyond. She had friends in multiple countries who helped relocate the women when they got them out of Turkey. Her network within the city passed on information about potential human sales or auctions. Miriam sent her people in to recover these people before they were sent to auction or sold. If she were too late for a preemptive move, they mounted surprise attacks as the women were loaded into transport vehicles.

Turkish law did not condone the sale of humans

or forcing them into marriages. However, the current administration had a tendency to overlook the rampant trade of female flesh within the country, doing little to stop it or curtail the flow. Miriam and her band of warriors did the best they could to fill in where the government failed.

Layla had huge admiration for Miriam and her cause. Her conversation with Hasan Saka had struck far too close to home. It made her feel like he might know something. That worried her. Why had he come to the US Embassy with the Minister of Justice that night? And why would he pin her down with questions about marriage and arranged marriages? Once she liberated her subject tonight, she'd find time to meet with Miriam and pass on the information about Hasan Saka. Right now, she just wanted to get to the woman being compromised, get her out, and get back to the embassy before she was missed.

Frankly, she was surprised that her current bodyguard hadn't noticed when she'd left her room. Her other two bodyguards would be on standby at the front entrance of the embassy, which was the only entrance open at this time of night. They'd fall asleep soon, but the front entrance was the only entrance. Layla had discovered the secret passage one day when she'd been in the library searching for a book. She'd been intrigued by the sconce on the wall. When she'd touched it and the bookshelf had moved, her imagination and curiosity had gotten the better of her. She'd followed the passageways all the way to the end in both directions. One led to the rooftop, presumably where a helicopter could lift the ambassador to safety, should the embassy be overrun. The lower route offered a more clandestine escape route, should they need one.

Layla had needed it and used it on many occasions, which frustrated her father to no end. He didn't know how she was getting out, or how she was getting past her bodyguards.

Following the GPS coordinates she'd been given, she slipped through the streets, clinging to shadows. The fewer people who saw her, the better. Not that they'd recognize her in the hoodie. She'd scrubbed her face free of makeup, in case she was caught. Thanks to her mother's genetics, Layla looked like any other Turkish woman, and she could speak the language. Her mother had seen to that. If anyone stopped her, she would just say, I'm on my way to see my grandmother who is sick.

She had been stopped one day by a police officer. She'd given that excuse, and he'd bought it, allowing her to pass with a warning that it wasn't safe for women to travel alone at night. She'd thanked him and moved on.

Now, she was thinking the officer had been right. Several times, she looked back, having the feeling that she was being followed. Occasionally, she heard footsteps, but when she turned, nobody was there. It was an unsettling feeling. If she was being followed and she was attacked, she had in her pocket a small can of mace. It wasn't much, but it might buy her time to escape if she sprayed it in his eyes. On the other hand, if he was following to see where she was going, that could cause problems in her attempt to liberate the woman targeted to be sold.

She ducked down an alley and zigzagged between buildings, trying to shake her tail, or at least shake that feeling that she was being tailed. She didn't have much time to get where she was going. Miriam had explained to her that it was a walled-in compound, but that it had a back gate. Unfortunately, it was kept locked.

Earlier that day Miriam's team had had a truck dump several pallets behind the wall to be used to scale the wall and drop onto the other side. The pallets could be turned sideways and used as a ladder to get over the wall. All she had to do was scale the wall and find the window with the peace sign drawn in the bottom right-hand corner of the glass. The subject would be watching for her. Layla carried a very small flashlight with a red lens. She'd blink that red flashlight three times in a row. The woman was to crawl out her window and follow the flashlight. Layla would help her over the fence, and they'd escape with nobody knowing the better. Until they came to find that the woman had gone.

That was all assuming that she'd reach the house

before the men came who were negotiating the sale of the woman with her father. It all sounded pretty easy to her. Timing would be the key.

Layla picked up her pace. When she could hide in the shadows, she ran. Otherwise, she walked fast to keep from drawing unwanted attention from anyone who might be out that late at night. As she neared her location, she studied her surroundings, searching for any vehicles hanging around, any people standing on the streets, or any lights shining from within the house.

Near the front of the house, a light shone through a window from what Layla could see without scaling the wall. She assumed it would be in the front living area where the father waited for the people who would come to claim their purchase.

Layla checked the time on her watch. She had thirty minutes to get this done. She prayed the men who were coming to claim this woman wouldn't show up any sooner.

The woman's name was Yara. When she'd been approached by one of the people in Miriam's network, Yara had had no clue that she was being sold. She couldn't believe her father would do such a thing. When her father told her he'd arranged a marriage for her, she'd become a believer and had gotten word to Miriam that she needed out of the country before midnight.

Layla circled to the back of the building, and as

expected, she found the pile of pallets. Again, she studied the area before she moved in and quietly layered the pallets, one at a time, making a taller stack so that she could stand on it and look over the edge of the wall. It was dark on the backside of the house. She laid over the top of the wall on her belly, reached down, and grabbed one of the pallets from the stack and pulled it over, easing it down on the other side. Leaning it against the wall would provide just enough of a ladder to get them high enough to where they could pull themselves up over the wall. Sliding over the top, she placed her foot on the top of the pallet and lowered herself down the ladder.

Once inside the wall, she inched around the building, looking for the window with the peace sign. Her heart pounded and her hands grew clammy. Every noise made her jump.

When she found the peace sign, she stood back in the shadows, turned on her flashlight, pointed the red beam at the window and flashed it three times. Then she waited, her heart pounding, her muscles bunched, ready to take flight.

Headlights flashed in the streets in front of the house, and an engine rumbled to a stop. Men's voices carried to where Layla stood in the yard. Her heart cartwheeled against her ribs. The woman's transport had arrived. They only had seconds to get Yara out. The window in front of her opened. A young girl's face appeared, her eyes round and frightened.

"Yara?" Layla whispered.

She nodded.

Layla waved for her to come through the window. The girl looked over her shoulder one last time. Then she stuck one foot out the window, followed by the other, and dropped to the ground. She wore dark pants, a dark shirt, and an equally dark beanie hat on her head. She didn't look any more than twelve years old.

Anger burned in Layla's gut. This girl's father was selling her, a child, and probably didn't even care where she was going. She could be slated to become some old man's wife to be used and abused or sold into a sex trade to be treated even worse.

Yara carried a backpack on her back and ran towards Layla.

Layla guided her toward the pallet ladder and urged her to climb up and over the fence. When the girl got to the top of the pallet, she was too short to reach the top of the fence.

Layla climbed up behind her and gave her a shove, sending her to the top of the wall. The girl slipped over the side and dropped down onto the stack of pallets.

Layla pulled herself up onto the wall and was about to drop down when she heard a shout through the open window of the girl's bedroom. Lights glared from the window. Men rushed to look out. Before she could slip over the top of the wall, she heard shouts in Turkish.

"Stop him!" they said.

Layla dropped to the ground, grabbed the girl's hand and ran back the direction she'd come. She rushed for the shadows and ran square into a hard wall of muscle.

Hands grabbed her arms. She struggled to free herself.

"Let me go!" she whispered furiously.

"Not until you tell me what's going on," a familiar voice said.

She looked up into the face of her fiancé.

"And who's this girl?" he demanded.

She shook her head. "No time to explain. We have to get out of here. Now."

More shouts sounded behind her.

Still, Bull stood stock still. "Not until you tell me what's going on."

"I'll tell you what's going on," she whispered. "Those men coming over the wall are going to kill us if we don't get out of here now."

His gaze went to the wall. A couple of men had started over the top.

"Okay, come with me." He took her hand.

With her other hand, Layla held onto the girl, and they ran, ducking between buildings, putting distance between them and the men who gave chase.

When it didn't appear they'd escape being caught,

Bull led them down an alley between two buildings where he found a door. He jiggled the handle. It was locked. He cocked his leg and kicked the door until it opened. Once inside, he shut it. They found themselves in an old warehouse filled with crates and boxes.

"Help me move that crate," he said. Between him and Layla, they pushed a crate in place, blocking the door.

Bull straightened and spun on his heel. "Now, let's find our way out the other side."

They crossed the building, weaving between more crates and boxes, passing a forklift until they reached the other side of the large warehouse. There wasn't another door on that side, and if they tried to go around the front then they might be seen on the street. The door they had blocked was being rattled at that point, and soon they could hear people banging against it, shoving the crate they'd used to block it out of the way.

"We're going up," Bull said, and led them up a metal staircase to the next level of the warehouse in the back. When they reached the top, he entered an office.

All Layla could think was that they were trapped.

Bull crossed the office and shoved a desk out of the way at the back, revealing a window. He opened it and looked out.

"We're in luck," he said. "There's a fire escape out

of this window. Let's go." He helped the girl through it, and then Layla, and then climbed out on the platform with them. The escape ladder had been pulled up and secured. He found the latch, released it, and pushed the ladder down. Bull went down first, the girl next and Layla last.

Once on the street, they ran again. They continued to run until Layla was positive that they'd lost the men who'd been following them. She slowed to a stop, breathing heavily, the girl beside her bending over to catch her breath.

"Now, maybe you can tell me what's going on?" Bull demanded.

She shook her head, got out her phone, checked for GPS coordinates of the transfer point and said, "We have to get to this location within the next thirty minutes."

He shook his head, crossing his arms over his chest. "I'm not going anywhere until you tell me what's going on."

"Fine, then stay here. I've got to get the girl to this location in the next thirty minutes." Layla started out on her own.

Bull caught up and grabbed her arm. "Who's this girl? What are you doing with her?"

"I'm saving her from a really crappy life," she said. "Now, you can either help me or get out of my way."

Bull stepped in front of her. "For all I know you could be kidnapping her. And her father might be calling the police right now to say that his daughter has been stolen from his home."

"Then perhaps he can explain why he was selling her to the highest bidder, and that bidder was coming tonight. In fact, that's who's been chasing us —the men who bought her from her father."

Bull turned to the girl. "Yara, do you speak English?"

Yara nodded. "I do." She faced Bull. "Everything she said is true. My father was selling me to those men. He told me it was an arranged marriage." She snorted. "I heard him talking on the phone. He sold me. It wasn't an arranged marriage. They were there to pick me up. I didn't want to go, but my father needed the money to support himself and my little brother. I just couldn't do it." Tears filled her eyes and spilled down her cheeks.

Bull looked from the girl back to Layla and sighed. "My gut tells me that what you're doing is illegal. And my gut tells me that what her father was doing was even more so. But he could always claim that he wasn't doing that."

"But he was," Yara insisted. "The men came two days ago. They made me strip." Her voice caught on a sob. "I was ashamed. I could not go with them. I would rather leave my family, leave my country and start over somewhere new, than go with those men."

"How old are you, Yara?" Bull asked.

She lifted her chin. "I'm eighteen. I look young for

my age."

"Do you have a passport?" he asked.

She shook her head. "My father wouldn't let me get one."

Bull looked at Layla. "How do you plan on getting her out of the country without a passport?"

Layla's eyes narrowed. "You don't have to worry about that. In fact, you don't have to worry about us anymore. Go back to the embassy. I'll return shortly."

He shook his head. "I can't. You're now my responsibility."

She frowned. "And I can't take you where I'm going."

"I guess we have a problem then, don't we? You won't go with me, and I won't let you go without me."

"And I only have thirty minutes to get this done," she reminded him.

His jaw firmed. "Then you're going to have to trust me to go with you."

"It's not whether or not I trust you." Layla stood toe to toe with Bull. "The people who are going to help Yara aren't going to trust you. They might disappear, and this operation will fall apart. Yara will end up back in her father's hands and be transferred over to these men who will sell her into some sleazy brothel. I can't let that happen."

"I won't go back," Yara said. "I'll find my own way out of the country." She turned and started to walk away.

"It's too dangerous to go on your own," Layla said. "Everything is arranged. We just have to get you to the right place at the right time." She sighed. "Fine. You can come with us, but when we get close, you'll have to hang back. I don't want the people that are taking Yara to get skittish."

"Lead the way," he said.

Layla followed the GPS directions, weaving through the streets until she came to the meeting location. She stopped short of the street where she would make the handoff to Miriam's team. Her people would take Yara to a safehouse, until she could be transported out of the country. Yes, it was illegal as hell, but it saved the women from a life worse than death.

"Is this it? Is this where they're going to pick her up?" Bull asked. "And who is they?"

"It's a team. A network of people who help relocate these women."

"How do you know they're not just selling them into another sex trade?"

Layla had thought about that. She'd used some of her contacts in the Secret Service to locate women they'd claimed to have saved. The women had been shipped to different countries, like France, the UK, Sweden and more. Her Secret Service contact had spoken to several of them and had assured Layla they were who they said they were and that they were healthy, happy and living full, free lives. "I have contacts who verified their stories."

Headlights flashed at the end of the street as a vehicle turned onto the road in front of the building where Layla, Yara and Bull hid. A white utility van raced toward them, pulling to a stop at the corner.

The door slid open, and Miriam Rogers poked out her head. She wore dark clothing and a black knit hat over her hair. "Yara," she called out.

Layla nodded to Yara. "This is it. Ready?"

Yara squeezed Layla's hand. "I'm ready."

Layla hurried out of the shadows toward the van with Yara's hand in hers.

"Get in," Miriam said.

Yara jumped into the van.

"You, too," Miriam said. "We've been tailed. Hurry."

"I'm not going with you."

More headlights swung onto the street several blocks away.

"Then run," Miriam shouted, closing the van door. The vehicle leaped forward, tires squealing against the pavement.

Layla ran back to the shadows. "Time to go," she said and ran in the same direction the van had gone.

Bull raced to catch up with her.

Layla and Bull had already reached the next corner and turned when a shout went up. As they rounded the side of a building, Layla looked back.

Two men had gotten out of the trailing vehicle and were running toward them. She cursed and picked up her speed.

Bull grabbed her hand, urging her faster.

Her legs ached, and her lungs burned, but she kept running.

Bull led her between different buildings, zigzagging in his attempt to lose the men behind them. When they came to a residential area, he slipped into a back alley, found a fence and catapulted her over it, and then vaulted over after her.

"Stay down," he said.

She lay on the ground in the shadows next to Bull, his arm over her, his body shielding hers. Footsteps pounded against the gravel in the alley as they neared. Layla held her breath, praying that they didn't stop at the fence, that they moved on. They slowed. The men spoke in Turkish. She caught a few of the words. They were questioning where they had gone. And then they were running again, leaving Layla and Bull behind.

When Layla started to get up, Bull's arm clamped around her. "Stay put for a few more minutes," he whispered.

She lay beneath his arm, aware of his warmth against her.

Footsteps sounded again, coming their direction. The men who had been chasing them were running back the other direction. Once again, they paused near the fence. One of them questioned the other that perhaps they'd hopped over a fence.

Layla's breath caught and held. They weren't that far away. If they looked over the fence at any point, they might spy them lying against the other side. One of them told the other to hop up on the fence and look over.

Bull's body bunched. He drew his legs up beneath him, ready to spring to her defense, if needed.

A shout in the distance caused the two men to stop talking. Then they were running again, away from them, back the direction they'd come. Layla let go of the breath she'd been holding.

Bull grabbed her arm and helped her to her feet. "Let's get out of here.". He looked over the top of the fence in both directions. "The coast is clear. Let's go." He again helped Layla over the fence and then vaulted over himself. They ran to the next street, turned and then ran some more.

When they were far enough away from where they'd been, they slowed to a walk. Layla removed her hoodie and tossed it in a trash bin.

She fluffed her hair out and gripped his hand. "If anybody stops us, we're just a couple out enjoying the night air," she said.

"Gotcha," he said. "Now, let's get back to the embassy so you can tell me what the hell this was all about, and why you're involved in an underground railroad."

CHAPTER 5

THINGS HADN'T GONE QUITE AS SMOOTHLY as Layla had anticipated. She had to admit that she was glad Bull had shown up when he had. Unfortunately, that meant that he knew what was going on, and that was one more person who knew about Miriam's operation.

"Do you know where you're headed now?" Bull asked her.

She glanced down at her cellphone map application and looked up at the street in front of her. "Back to the embassy compound, of course."

"How had you planned on getting back inside?"

She glanced up at him. "The same way I got out."

"I almost didn't find the lever in the wall sconce that opened the bookcase," he said. "It's a good thing I did."

She shot him an irritated glance. "I would've been

all right. I would've gotten Yara away from there without your help." She might have. Or not. However, if they had been caught, having a big guy like Bull had made her feel like she had a better chance of survival. Then again, she might not have thought to hide in the warehouse and escape through the upstairs fire escape. And she might not have been able to get herself over that fence to hide from the second round of guys who'd chased them. As much as she hated to admit it, Bull had come in handy that night.

"You realize I'll have to report this to your father, don't you?" he said.

Layla ground to a halt. "You can't tell my father. He can't know what I'm doing."

"He'll put a stop to it," Bull said.

"I won't stop doing this. Not as long as there are women who are being sold into the sex trade."

He gripped her elbow and continued their movement toward the embassy. "There have been women sold into the sex trade for centuries."

She jerked her arm free of his grasp. "That doesn't make it right."

"No, it doesn't, but you're not going to stop what's been going on for centuries. No one person could do that."

"I don't expect that I'll stop every occurrence, but if I can help one woman escape such a horrible fate, I've done more than most people."

He reached for her hand and held it firmly in his grip. "You'll end up in jail."

"I'm not going to jail, because they're not going to find out, and you're not going to tell my father."

As they continued walking, they were still holding hands like a happily engaged couple would. Layla would never tell him that she liked his big hand around hers or that it made her feel safe in a hostile environment.

"Look," Bull said, "my job is to keep you safe. I can't do my job if you're running off without me."

"Fine," she said. "I'll let you know whenever I go someplace."

He shook his head. "Sorry, sweetheart. I don't trust you."

She frowned. "Even if I give you my word?"

He shook his head. "Nope. I figure the only way I'm going to keep track of you is to be with you twenty-four-seven."

"Well, you are," she said.

"Not when you go off to your bedroom and I go off to mine," he pointed out. "I don't have you in sight."

She stopped and stared up at him, trying to pull her hand out of his grip. He held firm. "Are you suggesting that you sleep with me?"

"More or less," he said. "I'll sleep in the same room as you. The only time I'll have you out of my sight is when you walk into the bathroom. As long as the bathroom doesn't have a window exiting to the outside."

"That's ridiculous," she said. "No way am I agreeing to that."

He shrugged. "Fine, then I'll just tell your father about your little clandestine outings at night."

"You wouldn't," she said.

He nodded. "If you don't agree to my terms, I sure will."

"What if my dad finds out that you're sleeping in the same room as me?"

He smiled. "I'm betting your dad doesn't care as long as I keep an eye on you, and I don't hurt you."

Layla lifted her chin in challenge. "I could tell my dad that you hurt me, and he'd get rid of you in a heartbeat."

"And we're right back to the fact that I'll tell your dad about your night operations."

Layla tipped back her head and stared up at the sky. She drew in a deep breath and let it out on a huff. "Why do you have to be so obstinate?"

He snorted. "Why do you have to be involved in something that could ruin your father's career?"

Her head whipped around, and she stared into his eyes. "They needed me tonight. I don't usually get this close to the operations."

"You nearly got caught. And if you had been caught by these guys that are selling these girls into the sex trade, they would've turned around and sold you to the same place. You'd be gone. Your father would've lost you. Then he'd have no more family members to help support him or to love. How do you think he'd feel? Did he love your mother?"

"He did, with all his heart. It tore him up when she died." Layla stared at the street in front of her. "That's the major reason why I'm here. I didn't want him to go to his new assignment alone."

Bull looked down at her. "That would make you a commendable daughter, except for one thing."

She frowned. "And what's that?"

"Your clandestine operations," he said shaking his head as if talking to a child who couldn't quite understand.

"Who's gonna stick up for these women if I don't?" she whispered.

"Apparently, the team who has been rescuing them without your help until now."

"Yeah, but the more help they can get, the more women they can get out of that situation. If I hadn't gone tonight, Yara would've been on her way to some godforsaken hellhole, where men would treat her like a worthless piece of trash."

"So, what's it to be?" Bull challenged her.

Layla pulled her hand free of his and crossed her arms over her chest. "If I let you stay in my room, you will not be sleeping in my bed."

He nodded. "I didn't expect to. I assume you have

a suite like mine where you have a sitting area with a sofa?"

She nodded. "You could sleep on the sofa."

"Is there a window in your bathroom?"

She shook her head. "No."

"Okay then," he clapped his hands together, "I move in tonight."

Her eyes narrowed. "You step one foot over the line, and I don't care who you tell what I did tonight. I'll have my dad kick you out so fast."

"You're assuming I'm attracted to you."

Her eyes narrowed even farther into a squint. He couldn't have kissed her like he had and not felt something. Or was he that good an actor?

"Well, good then," she said, "because I'm not in the least attracted to you."

Okay, so that was a lie. How could she not be attracted to the man? He was incredibly sexy in a black suit, and he was strong and muscular in a way that was useful for keeping her safe. They walked a few more blocks with Layla following her GPS on her cellphone. As they approached the area with the hidden gate, Bull reached out and touched her arm.

"Wait." They'd stepped into the shadows of a building. Together, they studied the street and the surrounding buildings. Layla looked for any kind of movement indicating the presence of others.

"We might be better off going through the front gate tonight," Bull said.

"Why?" she asked.

"Twice tonight, we've been followed. It would be bad enough if they discovered that we were with the US Embassy, but it would be even worse if they found the secret tunnel leading to the interior."

She nodded. "Good point." Layla glanced around. "Do you think that we're being followed? Did you see anybody?"

He shook his head. "No. But better safe than sorry. Do you have your credentials on you?"

She nodded. "I don't carry a wallet, but I carry my papers in my bra." She fished them out. "Did you bring yours?"

He nodded.

"Then let's go around to the front of the building and enter like normal people," she said.

The guard at the gate checked their paperwork. They stepped through the scanner and were inside soon, taking the elevator to their floor. Bull stopped outside his door, opened it, and turned to her.

"Stay here." He entered, leaving the door wide open.

Layla tapped her foot, irritated that he didn't trust her for even a minute by herself.

Bull grabbed his suitcase, stuffed his shaving kit in it and returned to where she was standing in the hallway.

"You're really going to move in with me tonight, aren't you?" she said. She didn't quite like the thrill of excitement that rippled through her body. She doubted she'd get much sleep with him lying on the couch next to her bed. She wondered if he had pajamas to sleep in, or if he'd sleep in his boxers or briefs? The thought made heat coil low in her belly. The last thing she needed was to fantasize over whether he wore boxers or briefs.

She turned and led the way to her room, opening the door with her key.

Once inside, Bull turned and locked the door, closing them inside together.

A shiver of what felt like anticipation rippled down her spine. She went to the dresser, bypassed her usual nightgown, and dug in a drawer for a T-shirt and a pair of shorts and carried them into the bathroom. "I'll only be a minute."

Inside, she quickly brushed her teeth, pulled her hair back into a ponytail, and slipped out of her clothes and into the T-shirt and shorts. She splashed water on her face, dried off with a towel, and then stared at herself in the mirror for a short second. She looked about ten years younger with her hair in a ponytail. Not the least sophisticated. Not that Bull would care. Hadn't he said that he wasn't attracted to her? His kiss had only been an act.

Again, heat flared at her core. It might have been an act to him, but boy, she'd felt something. Not that she'd act on it. She exited the bathroom and found Bull waiting outside with his shaving kit in hand, a fresh T-shirt, and a pair of jogging shorts, which probably answered the question of what he'd be sleeping in. It wouldn't be in his boxers or briefs, unless they were underneath the shorts and T-shirt.

A fleeting sense of disappointment filled her, and she immediately brushed away. Having Bull in her room would be an inconvenience. Not a curiosity. Knowing whether he wore boxers or briefs was irrelevant. He was her bodyguard. She needed to keep that in mind and keep his hands off her.

And hers off him...

She turned on the light on the nightstand and turned off the overhead lights in the room. She found an extra blanket and pillow in the closet and laid them out on the couch for him. Then she crawled into bed and pulled the covers up over her bare legs. The sensation of the sheets sliding across her skin ignited her imagination, making her wonder what it would be like to have his hands on her bare legs. Those big strong hands that had held hers at different points during the night.

She laid back on the pillow and stared up at the ceiling, refusing to watch the bathroom door in anticipation of Bull emerging in her much-fantasized boxer shorts. She rolled over onto her side, turned away from the door, so that she wouldn't see him or be tempted to look. It wasn't as if she was interested in him. Yes, he kissed well, but she couldn't judge him based on one kiss alone.

The click of the door opening alerted her to his presence in the room. With the sound of rustling, she assumed he was putting something into his duffel bag. The creak of springs beneath the cushions on the couch indicated he'd settled in for the night.

Then silence.

Layla turned over to switch off the light and caught his gaze as he watched her.

"Please tell me you're not going to stare at me all night," she said.

He linked his hands behind his neck and shook his head. "I plan on being asleep in the next five minutes," he said. "You should sleep, too. I'm sure you have plans for tomorrow, which means I'll have plans for tomorrow." He closed his eyes.

"I have a scheduled visit with one of the orphanages and one of the elementary schools tomorrow here in Ankara."

With his eyes still closed, Bull nodded. "Sounds like fun. I like kids."

"I do, too." Layla stared up at the ceiling in the dark, unable to fall asleep. "Bull, have you ever been married?"

A soft snort sounded from the couch. "No."

"Why not?" she asked.

He chuckled. "Never had time to meet the right girl."

"So, you believe in marriage?"

"I do."

"That's sad," Layla said. "Not having time to find the right woman."

"It's the nature of the beast. I'm Delta Force. We deploy three-hundred-and-sixty-five days a year. Or at least it feels like it. It makes it hard to have any kind of relationship when you're never home."

"Makes sense," Layla said. "Have you ever been in love?"

"I thought I was once," Bull responded.

"What happened?"

"I deployed. We connected via internet for a while. That trickled off and, when I got back to the States, she had married somebody else."

"Well, that's depressing," Layla said.

"It's the reason I don't bother looking. I figure it isn't fair to a woman to be married to a Delta. She'd never see him. He'd never see her."

"A woman who is strong enough would understand," Layla said. "You're just not finding the right women."

He chuckled. "Women? I can't even find one woman, much less more. But it doesn't matter, I'm not looking. It's hard to maintain a relationship when you're always deployed."

"Well, you're deployed now, and look at us, already engaged." She laughed. "It's kind of like an arranged marriage, isn't it?"

"Well, it definitely wasn't a love match," he said.

"Get some sleep, Layla. You'll have a busy day tomorrow."

She lay for a moment, letting the silence grow between them. "Bull?"

"Yes, Layla."

"Thank you for helping me tonight."

"You're welcome."

Layla lay for another thirty minutes staring up at the ceiling, going over everything that had happened that evening. Nothing had gone quite right. But they had accomplished their mission and gotten Yara away from her father who was willing to sell her into the sex trade.

The sound of Bull's deep breathing made Layla feel safe and calm. At the same time, it made her body tense and disturbed. How could one man inspire both feelings that were diametrically opposed? He was irritating, yet he was sexy. And he'd more or less blackmailed her into letting him sleep in her room. For the right reason.

He had been tasked with protecting her. And the only way he could do that was be with her around the clock.

Layla finally closed her eyes and slept, dreaming of a man in boxer shorts, leaning over to kiss her as she lay naked in her bed.

. . .

ALL TOO SOON, morning sunlight filtered through her window around the blinds. She opened her eyes to find the couch empty and Bull gone. She sat up straight and looked around the empty room. So much for Bull keeping an eye on her. Then the bathroom door opened, and Bull stepped out, carrying his toiletries kit, his chin cleanly shaved.

"Rise and shine, sleepyhead," he said. "We have a full day ahead of us."

She groaned and pulled the comforter over her head to block out the sunlight and his cheerful disposition. She'd hated that he'd had the chance to sneak into the bathroom before her. She must be a mess with her ponytail hanging sideways, sleep in her eyes and morning breath.

"How are you for making coffee?" she asked from beneath the blanket.

"I've been known to make a pot or two," he said.

"There's a coffeemaker in the corner. Could you get some coffee started while I make use of the bathroom?"

"I can do that," he said, and strode to the other end of the room where the coffeemaker stood on the counter. Layla flung back the covers. She riffled through her dresser for a bra, went to her closet and pulled out a dress and hurried into the bathroom. One glance in the mirror confirmed her suspicion. She was a wreck.

Ten minutes later, with her hair neatly brushed, a

light dusting of makeup on her face, and wearing a light blue dress with short, capped sleeves, she emerged from the bathroom, feeling more confident and well put together. "I just have to put on shoes, and I'll be ready to go down for breakfast," she said.

He nodded and went to stand by the window, while she slipped a pair of strappy shoes on her feet.

A knock sounded on her door. Bull tensed and went to answer it. He pulled it open to find a woman standing there with a clipboard in her hand.

"Oh," she said, "I must have the wrong room." When she looked past him and saw Layla standing there buckling her shoes, she frowned. "I'm sorry, I didn't know you had company. I can come back later."

"That won't be necessary, Pinar," Layla said. "Pinar, you remember Greg Smith from last night? My fiancé." Layla nodded toward the man. "He'll be staying with me."

Pinar's eyes narrowed, and she nodded. "Very well, Ms. Grey. How long will he be with you?"

"I'm not certain." And she wasn't. How long did one borrow Delta Force soldiers for bodyguard duty?

Surely, it wouldn't be for long. They had better things to do, battles to fight, bad guys to ferret out. Babysitting an ambassador's daughter had to be the last thing he'd expected to do.

Layla hadn't wanted him in her life when her father had given her the edict that he was to be with her all the time. But now that she'd seen what he was capable of—and felt his kiss—she wasn't as anxious to be rid of him.

In fact, she was beginning to like the guy. Not that she'd ever tell him. Still, she wasn't ready for him to cut out. Life had begun to be a lot more interesting with Bull around.

CHAPTER 6

BULL HADN'T SLEPT MUCH the night before. The hard lumpy sofa wasn't nearly as unsettling as the thought of Layla lying in the bed a few short steps away.

If he could keep an eye on her without being in the same room, he might have slept better.

Hearing the whispery soft sound of her breathing and the occasional moan from her direction had his senses tied in knots and his groin so tight he could barely move.

Sleep finally claimed him around two in the morning. The sun, finding its way around the edges of the blinds in the window, woke him well before six o'clock, ending a restless night. He'd opted for a shower to wake him and a chance to shave.

When he stepped out of the bathroom, he felt more together, until he spotted Layla stretching in her bed, her hair messy and her face flushed pink with sleep.

His heart stuttered, and his pulse blasted through his veins.

When she'd asked for coffee, he would have given her the moon if that was what she'd requested.

What was wrong with him? He was Delta Force. Layla was an ambassador's daughter. If something grew out of their time together, how often would he be in Turkey to see her?

Never.

The woman standing at the door of Layla's quarters cocked an eyebrow as she stared at Bull. "Will you need your assigned quarters?" she asked. "Should I free it for others to use?"

"No," Layla said.

"Yes," Bull spoke at the same time. He overrode her with, "I'll room with my fiancée for the remainder of my stay in Turkey, however long that might be." He stared down at the woman, giving her a level, yet firm look that didn't invite further comment or query.

Ms. Erim's brow dipped. "I see."

"What is it you needed, Pinar?" Layla stepped up beside Bull.

"I wanted to go over your schedule for the day. It can wait until after breakfast. However, you have an early morning visit at the orphanage. They expect you at 9:00 am."

"We'll be there," Layla said. "Be sure to notify them that I'll be bringing my fiancé with me to meet the children. Did the boxes of toys arrive?"

Ms. Erim nodded. "They came in yesterday. We've loaded them into the van that will deliver them and you to the orphanage. It will be waiting out front when you're ready to leave."

"Thank you," Layla said.

At that point, the woman didn't seem inclined to leave.

"Is there anything else?" Layla asked.

"Yes, Ms. Grey." Ms. Erim glanced down at the organizer in her hands. "Don't forget you are expected at the international reception at the Grand Ankara Hotel."

"See that Mr. Smith is on the guest list. For that matter, now that he's here, I won't attend functions alone. Be sure that invitations extended to the ambassador and his daughter include an invitation to my fiancé."

Ms. Erim's brow remained furrowed as she scribbled a note into the notebook organizer.

"Is there anything else?" Layla asked.

Ms. Erim snapped her notebook shut. "No, Ms. Grey. I'll take care of the invitation and notify the orphanage of the change of plans."

"Thank you." Layla walked Ms. Erim through the door. "We'll be down for breakfast momentarily." She backed into her room and closed the door.

"I get the feeling Ms. Erim wasn't happy to see me in your suite."

"Frankly, it's none of her business who stays in my quarters with me."

"Do I detect friction between the two of you?" Bull slipped a belt through the loops on his trousers and buckled it in front.

"Ms. Erim has been at the embassy since before my father and I arrived. We kind of inherited her. The previous ambassador's wife spoke highly of her. She's good at keeping my schedule and does what I ask of her." Layla's brow dipped. "She's just never warmed up to me. I think she likes working with older women."

"Do you think she feels somewhat threatened by you?"

Layla shrugged. "I don't know why. I've never done anything to anger her, that I know of."

"Are you ready?" Bull asked.

Layla nodded.

Her pale blue dress fit her to perfection, accentuating the narrowness of her waist and the curves of her breasts and hips. The silvery high-heeled sandals showed off her trim ankles and the tightness of her calves. She was stunning.

"Do I look all right to visit the orphans?"

"You're gorgeous. Are you sure you're not going out to meet with the royals?"

She laughed. "Sometimes, I like to dress for the

orphans. They love to see pretty things. And in the box of toys, I've included balls, dolls and dress-up clothes for both boys and girls. We have tea parties, and I teach them how to be ladies and gentlemen."

Bull could imagine the children flocking around the pretty ambassador's daughter, in awe of her beauty.

"Other times, I go in my jeans and a baseball jersey. We have game day where I teach them about soccer, baseball, football, cricket and other sports."

"Which days do they prefer? Sport day or dress-up day?"

She laughed. "They love both equally. When we have sports day, they beg for dress-up day next. And vice versa."

He opened the door, stepped out into the hallway and offered her his arm.

She slipped her hand through the crook of his elbow and smiled up at him. "You're going to love the children."

"I already do."

They made it to dining room for breakfast with other members of the embassy staff where the ambassador discussed the business of the day and his plans.

As soon as breakfast was over, Bull and Layla returned to their room. While Layla was in the bathroom refreshing her makeup and brushing her teeth,

Bull sent a text to Rucker informing him of where they were headed that morning.

Rucker: Will send a couple of the guys for backup

Bull: Could have used that backup last night

Rucker: ?

Bull: Will fill you in later

Layla chose that moment to emerge from the bathroom. "Your turn," she said.

He tucked his cellphone into his pocket and entered the bathroom, leaving the door open while he brushed his teeth.

"Have you ever considered working full time for an embassy?" she asked him, as he brushed and rinsed.

He shook his head, stowed his toothbrush and dried his hands. "No. I never considered it. I like the brotherhood and camaraderie of the Delta Force. And I enjoy the challenge of our assignments."

She smiled. "Like this one?"

"I have to admit, this is the first one of this type that I've been involved with. But that's what I mean. Our missions are varied, which keeps it interesting."

"And dangerous," she said.

"Not all embassies have had it easy," Bull said. "This one's in a country right now full of strife. You don't know what's going to happen with the president, or the people who are rebelling against him."

She nodded. "True."

"Unfortunately, the embassy staff isn't combat trained to defend themselves."

"We have military personnel stationed here to provide our protection," she said.

His jaw tightened. "Not enough to repel a full-on attack."

"That's true," she said. "That's why we rely on our intel to stay ahead of such things."

He captured her gaze. "Intel didn't save the lives of the embassy staff in Libya."

Layla nodded. "You make a good point." She glanced at her watch. "And I'd love to debate the subject with you, but right now we have an orphanage to visit, and we need to get a move on if we're going to get there on time."

A van filled with boxes and driven by a member of the Turkish guard awaited them in front of the embassy. They traveled through the busy streets of Ankara to the orphanage where the staff of the orphanage met them with smiles and hugs.

Layla spoke to them in Turkish. They laughed and smiled and looked toward Bull. Layla showed them the ring on her finger, and she was greeted with more smiles and hugs. The orphanage staff and some of the older children carried boxes into the orphanage. Inside, the children were allowed to help empty the boxes and distribute the toys and dress up clothes. One of the staff members pulled Layla aside and spoke with her for a few minutes. Layla came back and smiled at Bull.

"The staff and the children have requested a special lesson in dancing. I don't suppose you know how to waltz. Did your cotillion preparation teach you that?"

Bull groaned. "As a matter of fact, yes, it did."

"Good, then we'll teach them how to waltz."

"On one condition," he said.

"And what's that?"

"We also teach them how to do a line dance. Though I was trained in ballroom dancing, I prefer country and western music two-stepping, and I can also do a little bit of line dancing."

Layla smiled. "That would be perfect. The children will love it."

As the staff cleared the dining room floor of tables and chairs and brought in a radio and speaker and tuned it to a local classical channel, Layla helped the children dress. The girls put on the princess dresses, and the boys scrambled to find jackets and trousers. When they were all dressed, Layla and the staff members paired them off —boy, girl, boy, girl. The orphanage director found a waltz on the radio and turned up the volume.

Layla stood in front of the girls and held her arms up in the position to dance.

Bull stood in front of the boys with one arm held low, the other arm held high, and then he stepped toward Layla, and put his hand around her, resting it at the middle of her back.

She placed her hand on his shoulder, and he held her other hand lightly in his palm. They waited for the children to assume the same position with their partners. Then using very deliberate steps, Bull led Layla in the 1-2-3 step of the waltz, counting out loud.

"1-2-3, 1-2-3." He danced her around the room and came to a stop back where he had started. She had followed him perfectly, her body moving in time to his. He wanted to keep going, but the children were anxious to try their hand at it. Layla took one young couple—the children were perhaps ten, maybe twelve years old—and she helped them to move to the 1-2-3 step, until they had it down and sailed across the floor on their own.

Bull chose another couple, a little younger, probably eight or nine, and showed them how to perform the steps. The boy and girl moved in jerky motions but had the steps down, if not in time to the music. Soon, all the little couples were moving about the floor. Some concentrated on their steps, counting out loud. Others laughed and rocked back and forth, clueless about the proper way to waltz, but having fun anyway.

When the music stopped, the children dropped their holds and clapped, begging for more.

Bull crossed to the radio, spun the dial and found

a country and western station. He hurried back to the front of the room and turned his back to the others. Moving slowly, making his footwork overly obvious, he showed them one step after the other. It was a simple line dance with only a few different movements. Soon, the children had it mastered.

When the song came to an end, the children all shouted for more. They danced to several songs with the same line dance. By then it was time for the children to eat their lunch and for Bull and Layla to leave. Everyone pitched in to help the staff move the tables and chairs back to their positions.

The children gathered around Bull and Layla, all talking at once and reaching out for hugs, which Layla gladly gave them. Bull got down on his knees to hug some of the littler ones. He hadn't realized how much he missed children.

He glanced over a Layla. One little girl did not want to let go of her leg. Others touched her dress, loving the feel of it. The children loved her, and Layla was so good with them. But it was time for them to go.

When they stepped outside of the orphanage, Layla leaned into the van and spoke to the driver. He nodded.

She looked out at Bull. "Do you mind if we walk a little of the way? We can catch a cab back to the embassy."

He wasn't sure he liked that idea. It left her too

exposed. But hell, they'd gone all through the city at night, and this was daytime, what could happen?

In his experience, a lot, but it was a beautiful day. The sun was shining, and he liked the idea of walking with her.

She had her two bodyguards lurking nearby, and Rucker had promised a couple of the guys as Bull's backup.

He looked around searching for them. It took him a moment to find them. As promised, they were there.

Mac leaned against a lamp post with a newspaper in his hand, pretending to read the pages. Dawg sat on a low wall bouncing a tennis ball between his knees.

Bull had the backup he needed, and they'd follow. He smiled at Layla. "Okay, let's walk."

She waved the van driver off, and he left the building in the empty van and drove away.

"Do you know where we're walking?" Bull asked.

Layla nodded as she strolled along at an easy pace. "If we stay on this road, we'll eventually come to the downtown area with all the shops. We can do a little window shopping before we have to head back to the embassy."

After they had gone several blocks, Bull glanced back. Mac and Dawg followed at a staggered distance. The closer they got to the town center, the more people who were on the street.

Bull felt his phone vibrate in his pocket, and he pulled it out. It was Mac texting him.

Mac: You've got a tail

Bull moved closer to Layla and rested his hand at the small of her back. He leaned close as if he wanted to kiss her ear. Instead, he whispered, "Somebody's following us."

She looked up at him sharply. "How do you know?"

"Two of my guys have spotted him." Bull pressed his lips to her temple.

Layla closed her eyes and leaned into him. "Your guys are following us?"

He nodded, "Yes. As soon as I knew we were going to the orphanage, I reported to my team the location. They sent two guys as backup."

"That's good to know. I didn't even know your team was in the country." Layla's lips twisted. "Why am I always the last to know? First you, then your team…"

"It's all on a need-to-know basis." He winked.

Her lips firmed into a straight line. "So, who's following us?"

"I don't know, but we need to move a little faster." He pressed his hand to the small of her back and urged her to pick up the pace.

"Would it help if we ducked into one of the shops?" she asked.

He shook his head. "It would help more if we put

some distance between us, and then catch a cab back to the embassy."

"If we have one person following us, how do we know that we don't have more than one?" She nodded toward the crowded streets ahead. "There are a lot of people out here."

His body tensed. With so many people on the streets, it was inevitable they'd bump into a few. He hoped they didn't bump into anyone with a weapon. "We don't know how many are following us, therefore, it would be a good idea to find that cab."

"But that would slow us down as well." Layla nodded toward the people ahead of her. "It looks like some kind of gathering. Maybe we could lose ourselves in the crowd, and then duck out and find a cab."

His cellphone vibrated again.

Mac: We're now up to three people interested in you two.

Mac: We're moving in. Head for the crowd. We've got your back.

Because she was wearing high-heeled sandals, Layla couldn't move as fast as Bull. He took that into account but encouraged her to walk as fast as she could. The sooner they merged into the crowd, the sooner they could get lost in it. They'd have to get deep into the throng before they could get lost. Because she was wearing the pale blue dress, she would be easy to spot until then.

The crowd thickened, and many were chanting.

"What are they saying?" Bull asked.

She glanced up at her eyes widening. "They're protesting the president. It's an anti-government demonstration. This might not be the crowd to get lost in."

"We don't have much choice right now." Bull grabbed her hand and pulled her behind him, weaving between people who shouted and raised their fists.

Some carried signs, others carried rocks or bricks in their hands. The chanting grew louder, and the crowd thickened until Bull and Layla were pushed along with them.

Bull held tightly to Layla's hand, afraid that she would be torn away from him if he didn't. A shout ahead made him look over the top of the heads of the others in front of him. Women and men screamed and yelled.

A phalanx of Turkish military pushed toward the throng of anti-government demonstrators, carrying shields. People around Bull and Layla hurled their rocks and bricks at the shields.

Bull had to get Layla out of there quickly before the Turkish military decided to open fire on the crowd. The problem was that the crowd that had surged forward was now being pushed back, making it nearly impossible for Bull and Layla to move any direction. He pulled her into the circle of his arms and kept her as close as he could to keep her from being crushed. Just when he thought that they wouldn't make it out of there, someone grabbed his arm.

"Come on, we're getting you out of here," Mac said.

Between Mac, Dawg and Bull, they shoved and pushed their way to the edge of the crowd and escaped down a side street, moving quickly to get as far away from the demonstration as they could before the Turkish police took matters into their own hands. They ran, and Layla kept up with them, even in her high heels. When they had gotten far enough away that the crowd had thinned, they slowed to a walk.

Mac dropped back, making sure that their tail hadn't found them.

Dawg moved forward.

Ahead of them, Dawg waved down a cab and had the door open and ready for when Bull and Layla reached it. Layla got in and slid all the way across. Bull got in after and made room for Dawg and Mac.

Dawg shook his head. "You guys go on without us. Mac and I will catch another cab back to the hotel."

The cab moved slowly through the crowded streets until the crowds thinned even more and the driver was able to increase their speed to faster than a slow jog.

Only then did Bull relax, just a little. "Okay, in hindsight that might not have been a good idea to get lost in the crowd."

Layla leaned back against the seat and laughed. "That might be an understatement. Thank you for getting me out of there. And please, tell your guys thanks for helping. That was pretty intense," she said.

He nodded and reached for her hand. She held on to his for the rest of the journey back to the embassy. He hadn't liked that she'd been in danger. Not only from the men tailing her but also from being crushed in a crowd or trampled by the Turkish military.

When they arrived at the embassy, they passed through the screening at the gate and entered the building. Layla's father met them in the lobby. He grabbed Layla's hands and held them.

"Why didn't you ride back in the van? When it came back without you, I was so worried." He glared at Bull.

"It's okay, Daddy. We walked for a short distance, and then caught a cab to get the rest of the way back." She smiled reassuringly at her father. "It was such a pretty day, and I wanted to do some window shopping."

Her father held both of her hands in his. "But there was a riot downtown. I heard it on the news, and when you didn't come back, I was so worried."

She squeezed his hands. "But you see I'm okay."

He hugged her to him. "Maybe I should send you back to the States."

Layla raised her eyebrows. "Just because I didn't take the van back to the embassy?"

"No, that's not it. Things are just getting so volatile around here." He smiled down at her. "I worry that you'll get caught up in it."

"Daddy, I'm a grown woman," she said softly. "And I make my own decisions. Please don't try to make them for me."

He shook his head. "You're my only family."

"And you're mine," she said. "And that's why I'm here with you."

"As much as I love having you here with me, I'd feel better if you were safe back in the United States."

Layla shook her head. "And I'd feel better staying right here and making sure that *you're* okay."

"Sweetheart, you can't live your life for me. You need to have a life of your own."

"Daddy, I'm happy with what I do. I like being here for you, and the work is interesting and rewarding."

Her father frowned. "Maybe we should call off going to the event tonight. Especially after the demonstration today."

"I'm sure by now the riot has been controlled." Layla touched her father's arm. "It's a fundraising event for children with cancer, and all of the embassies' ambassadors have been invited, as well as many of the Turkish government officials. We have to be there."

"I don't know," he said. "There's so much unrest."

"We'll be all right." She smiled and patted his arm. "We're going. Now, I'm going to go rest for a little while so that I'll be fresh for the evening's gala. I've been on my feet in these high heels for far too long." She smiled at her father and gave him a hug. "We're going to be all right."

Her father kissed her forehead. "You look so much like your mother. Sometimes, it breaks my heart."

"She loved you so much," Layla said.

"And you," her father said. "Go. Get that rest you need. I have some work to do, and then I might follow your lead and get some rest before tonight's event as well."

Bull reached for Layla's hand as they strode to the elevator. He envied the love she and her father had for each other. It made him miss his mother and father so much his chest hurt. As an only child, he'd been very close to both of them. His father had died of a heart attack when he'd been only forty-eight. His mother had passed soon after with cancer. Bull thought she'd died more from a broken heart than cancer. He'd give anything to have them back.

When they reached the room, Layla gathered a T-shirt and some shorts and headed for the shower.

Bull texted Rucker.

Bull: Mac and Dawg make it back?

Rucker: Affirmative

Bull: Fundraiser at the Grand Ankara Hotel tonight

Rucker: Already received orders to cover the event

Bull: From?

Rucker: Your boss

Rucker: The gang will all be there

Bull: Good to know

Rucker: Three inside, four outside

Bull: See ya there

Rucker: Out

Feeling a little better about going to the fundraising gala that night, Bull kicked off his shoes and relaxed on the couch, feeling instantly sleepy. He must've been more exhausted than he'd thought. He'd need to be on his toes that evening in order to keep Layla safe.

If somebody had been following them that day, they might attempt to get into the event that night. He refused to let anything happen to Layla. He'd hate for her father to lose another loved one. And Bull would personally hate to lose Layla. The woman was growing on him.

He closed his eyes for a moment. Before he knew it, he was asleep.

CHAPTER 7

LAYLA STOOD IN THE SHOWER, letting the hot water rush down over her and soothe her tense muscles. As she stood naked in the water, she imagined Bull joining her. She had seen a side of him today that made her appreciate him even more. The man was good with children. He liked them, and they liked him. He'd make a good father.

She squirted liquid soap onto her hands, rubbed them together to lather up, and then ran them over her body, wishing they were Bull's hands, not hers. The thought made her hands stop midway down her torso. He wasn't her real fiancé. He was her bodyguard. She shouldn't be having such sensual thoughts about the man. To him, she was an assignment.

To her, he was one hundred percent ruggedly sexy male who could kiss like nobody's business.

Was she feeling this way because it had been a long time since she'd had a date?

She shook her head. No, it wasn't because she hadn't had a date. She wasn't desperate. It was Bull. He was the reason she was feeling this way. He was tough when he had to be; he'd proven that by making it through the Delta training. He'd proven it again by getting her out of the situation last night and today. And yet, he'd been gentle and kind and caring toward the children at the orphanage, and toward her.

And that kiss last night... Why couldn't she shake it from her mind?

Because it had felt so good. So good that she wanted to do it again. She let her hand trail over her breasts and down to the juncture of her thighs. What would it feel like to be with Bull? To feel his body naked against hers?

Heat built at her center and spread throughout her body. She slipped her hand lower, parting her folds to touch herself there. Her breath hitched, and her pulse quickened.

What if she opened the bathroom door and invited Bull to join her? Would he?

Layla moaned. Fantasizing was doing her absolutely no good.

She turned the water to the cold setting, hoping to chill the heat inside her. She rinsed off the suds and left the shower. After she dried off, she slipped her T-shirt over her head and pulled on her shorts.

When she stepped out of the bathroom, the first thing she saw was Bull with his head leaned back on the couch, his eyes closed. He was asleep, and she had all the time she needed to study him.

Bull wasn't handsome in a movie star kind of way. Instead, he was ruggedly handsome like a cowboy who worked in the outdoors. What would he do if she went to him, straddled his hips and kissed him? The thought was so titillating, she found herself moving toward him. When she stood in front of him, his eyes opened.

Heat rushed up her neck and into her cheeks.

Bull smiled and held out his hand.

Layla took it automatically and let him draw her closer to where she stood between his knees.

"I was just dreaming about you," he said.

Her breath caught. "You were?"

He nodded. "I dreamed that I was kissing you."

"And did I kiss you back?" she asked.

He nodded and tugged her arm gently until she sat in his lap. "I know this is wrong, and it's not part of my job description," he said, "but I just can't resist." He pulled her close, cupped her check in his hand and bent to take her lips with his.

She melted against him, slipped her arm around his shoulders and drew him closer. Her cool skin heated against his, and she opened, thrusting her tongue out to meet his. Kissing him was great but, oh, she wanted so much more. With her free hand, she guided his hand to her hip and slid it beneath her T-shirt.

Bull took over from there, sliding his hand across her skin and up to cup her breast. She arched her back, pressing herself into his palm and deepening their kiss at the same time.

This was where she'd wanted to be since last night's kiss. Her desire had been more of an ache that she couldn't put a finger on. Now, she recognized it for what it was. She wanted him to make love to her. She broke off the kiss, cupped his cheeks in her palms and stared into his eyes. "This isn't enough."

Bull frowned. "I don't understand."

"I want more," she said.

His eyes narrowed. "We shouldn't even be doing this."

She smiled. "But it's like you said...I can't resist. And why should I?" She held up her hand with the ring on her finger, her smile broadening. "After all, we're engaged."

He shook his head. "Not for real."

"It's real enough for me," she said.

"And when I leave?" he asked.

"I won't expect you to call me, if that's what you mean."

"I'm Delta," he said.

"I'm not asking for forever," she said, "just this moment." She climbed off his lap and held out her hand.

He took hers in his and let her draw him to his feet. She led him to the bed and stood in front of him as she pulled her T-shirt over her head.

He closed his eyes and moaned. "Are you sure about this?" he said. "Because once we start, I don't know that I can stop."

"Please," she said, "don't stop."

Layla reached for the buttons on his shirt and loosened them one at a time, yanking the tail from the waistband of his trousers. Then she unbuckled his belt and pulled it free of the loops, freed the button on his waistband and dropped the zipper.

His erection sprang free into the palm of her hand, and she felt an odd sense of power. She'd done this. She'd inspired this. Lord help her, she wanted him inside her. Now.

In the next two seconds he kicked off his shoes, his trousers and his boxer shorts, while she slipped out of her gym shorts. Then they were both on the bed lying beside each other, exploring with their mouths and their hands. Every inch.

"Please," she begged, "I need you inside me."

He chuckled. "Not yet."

"I don't know if I can wait," she said.

"Look, if I can wait, so can you. I want you to be as ready as I am when the time comes."

"I'm ready," she insisted.

"No, you only think you are." And he started to prove himself right by kissing her lips, and then trailing his mouth across her chin and down the long line of her neck. He paused at the base of her throat and kissed the pulse hammering there. Then he moved lower, captured one of her breasts between his teeth and rolled the nipple until it beaded into a hard little bud. He switched to the other and flicked his tongue across it, until she writhed and arched her back.

"Please," she moaned.

"Soon," he promised, and continued his downward path, leaving a trail of kisses across her ribs, angling lower until he reached that tuft of hair at the juncture of her thighs.

What he was doing to her…what she wanted him to do…

Bull parted her folds and touched his tongue to that nubbin of flesh so tightly packed with the nerves that the simple action set her entire body on fire.

Layla cried out and dug her fingers into the comforter beneath her, trying to ground herself when she was shooting to the stars.

When he touched her again, she spiraled out of control as she rocketed to the heavens. For a long, breath-stealing moment, she rode the rocket to the moon and back, her body pulsing with her release.

When she finally came back to earth, she wove her hands into his hair and tugged. He climbed up her body and kissed her full on the lips then rolled away from her and off the bed.

"Where are you going?" she asked.

"A wise man told me to always be prepared." He reached into his shaving kit, pulled out a small packet and carried it back to the bed.

"I'm glad one of us is thinking," she said.

He chuckled, tore open the packet and rolled it down over himself. Then he settled between her legs and kissed her again. She grabbed his buttocks and guided him to her entrance.

He paused, his engorged staff pressing her there, a portent for pleasure to come.

"Don't tease," Layla said, barely able to catch her breath.

He dipped into her as if testing how tight and wet she was. She was both.

And he felt so good inside her. Layla was past waiting, past testing and ready. She gripped his hips and brought him home.

He paused, buried deep in her channel.

She adjusted to his girth, reveling in how he filled her to full and then some.

Then he began to move. Slowly at first, rocking in and out of her, building his pace, increasing the intensity of his thrusts.

Layla's breathing became ragged, her body an inferno of desire. She planted her heels on the mattress and rose to meet him.

Soon, he was pumping in and out of her, fast, hard and deep.

When she thought she might come apart, Layla burst over the edge, threw back her head and called out his name. "Greg!"

Bull rode her one last time, driving deep and true. He remained there, his cock pulsing inside her, his body tense above hers.

Together, they soared to the stars.

When they came back to their senses, Bull dropped down on top of her and rolled them both to their sides, maintaining their connection. He kissed her gently and cupped her cheek.

"So much for a nap," she sighed and snuggled against him. "I think we have enough time for thirty minutes. Although our mattress gymnastics was invigorating enough to recharge me."

He chuckled and reached for his watch. "I'll set my watch for thirty minutes. Close your eyes."

She did and rested her cheek against his chest. "Maybe my dad was right, and we shouldn't go to this event tonight."

Bull kissed her temple. "I could think of a lot more things I'd rather do than go to an event with a lot of ambassadors and Turkish politicians."

She sighed. "But that's the nature of our job." She rested her hand on his bare chest, loving the feeling of all the muscles beneath her fingertips. "I'd skip it if I could."

"Then we'll go," he said, "but you can sleep for thirty minutes. My alarm will wake us."

She felt warm and safe and so complete lying in Bull's arms. But sleep was the farthest thing from her mind. As she lay there, her body heated again. She trailed her fingers over his chest and down lower.

Cupping his buttocks, Layla rocked her hips. She could feel him harden inside her.

They spent the twenty minutes making love again. Afterward, they slipped into the shower to rinse off before they had to get dressed for the evening. Making love in the shower was an entirely different, sweet assault on her senses.

When they finished, her knees were weak, and she couldn't stop smiling. The water grew cold, forcing them to leave the shower and towel each other dry before they dressed.

"You know you're not obligated to do this again," Layla said, pulling panties up her thighs and hips. "But it felt so good. I wouldn't object to a repeat performance."

He laughed. "Sweetheart, I wasn't obligated to do it the first time or the second time, for that matter." He pulled her into his arms and kissed her. "I wanted to do what we did just as badly as you."

She looked up into his eyes. "And after this evening's affair?"

He grinned. "I'm game if you are."

Her smile matched his. "Let's hope it ends early."

He slapped her on the butt. "Then we'd better get there."

She couldn't wipe the grin off her face as she dressed. And she was still smiling when they climbed into the car that would carry them to the hotel.

AFTER MAKING love two times in the bed and one time in the shower, Bull sure could have used that thirty-minute nap before they started getting ready to go to the fundraising gala.

Layla shooed him out of the bathroom so she could get ready, taking her dress with her. The garment had been wrapped in a dry-cleaning bag so he couldn't even tell what color it was. She wanted to surprise him.

While she got ready in the bathroom he dressed in the main room. Then he texted Rucker to see how things were going with their preparations to join him at the event.

Bull: Getting ready?

Rucker: Working on it. Didn't anticipate the need for four of us to dress formal. Scrambling, but we found suits in time

Bull chuckled. He could picture the others rushing around town, trying to find suitable attire for a formal event.

Bull: Who's designated inside?

Rucker: Mac, Blade and yours truly. Dawg, Tank, Dash and Lance have perimeter, keeping tabs of people coming and going

Bull smiled. Those were the people he would've chosen to come inside and pull perimeter duty. Well, maybe not Blade. He'd be too busy flirting with the women to notice anything untoward happening.

Rucker: Don't forget your communications devices

Bull: Got 'em

Rucker: Stay vigilant

Bull: Roger. Out

It would be nice to be plugged in with his team throughout the evening, knowing they were there and could hear him if he needed them. And they'd be his extra set of eyes and ears as well as having his back.

Bull was concerned about the evening's events. Any time there were that many foreign dignitaries and government officials in one place, things could happen. He just hoped that if things went down, he could get Layla and her father out before the shit hit the fan.

Bull: What do you know about the outcome of the riot earlier today?

Rucker: Turkish military quelled the uprising. Nearly one-hundred people were arrested or detained.

Bull: That's a lot.

Rucker: You were lucky to get out. Five people died. One crushed to death, four fired upon by Turkish military upon the president's orders

Bull's chest tightened. The people of Turkey wanted change. The president had control of the military. If the people wanted change, blood would be spilled. Bull hoped he could keep Layla out of that line of fire.

But the route she'd chosen was dangerous in itself. Somehow, he had to convince her not to participate with the underground railroad again.

One step at a time.

He had to get her through this evening's gala and back to the embassy alive.

His pulse quickened as he thought about what would happen after they got back to the embassy. He couldn't believe she'd been standing there in front of him when she'd come out of the bathroom earlier. She'd been ready and willing to make love with him. He'd been dreaming about her, about the kiss and wanting more. It was as if he'd been woken from his dream but was still in it when she'd climbed into his lap and kissed him.

For a man who'd sworn off relationships, he was falling deeply into this one. He hoped she fully understood what being a Delta meant. The Army owned him. He had to go when he was called. As much as he'd want to stay with her, he'd have to go. There was no future for them.

Images of her playing with the children at the orphanage flashed through his mind. She would make a great mother. She would be good with her own children, and they'd love her dearly. Bull found himself envying the man who would give her those children. Hell, he wanted it to be him. He could imagine little dark-haired, dark-eyed girls. Looking just like Layla, they'd run up to him, wrap their arms around his knees and beg him to lift them into the air.

Or little boys just as dark-haired and dark-eyed, bringing him a baseball glove and asking him to throw a ball with them. How he'd love to teach a little boy how to play baseball or football or go camping and fishing, as his father had done with him.

He found himself envying a life he couldn't have. A life he really wanted. Until that moment, he'd never regretted joining Delta Force. But now, he second-guessed his decision. Yes, he loved the brotherhood, and he'd do anything for the men on his team.

Bull turned as Layla stepped out of the bathroom fully dressed, her hair pulled up in a loose bun on top of her head, tendrils falling down around her ears. She wore a shiny silver dress that clung to her curves and fell to the floor in silken waves. A diamond necklace graced her neck and diamonds glittered in her earlobes.

Bull wanted nothing more than to drink her in, strip her naked and take her back to bed. "Wow," he said.

Her smile lit the room. "You like it?"

He nodded and held out his hand. "Very much so. I didn't know a woman could be this beautiful."

Her cheeks flushed a pretty pink. "Thank you."

"I don't suppose you'd consider staying here after all?" he asked.

"In a heartbeat," she said.

He sighed. "Damn. I'm committed to getting you there. If we choose to stay, your father will come looking for us."

"True," she said. "I could pretend that I have a cold." She covered her mouth and coughed delicately.

Bull shook his head. "But you won't. You convinced your father this gala was important. And if he's there, you'll be there, too."

She shook her head. "The life of an ambassador is a commitment. Your time is not your own."

"But you're not the ambassador," he pointed out.

"No, but when I came with my father, I committed to being his plus one and the hostess to the US embassy."

Bull shook his head. "Even if we wanted to make a go of a relationship between you and me, it would be doomed from the start."

She nodded. "I know. You're a Delta, you deploy. I'm the daughter of an ambassador. A *widowed* ambassador. I'm committed to being here. Once your assignment is over," she said, "you'll be gone. You won't have any reason to come back."

He took her hand and pulled her into his arms. "I

wouldn't say that. I'd have plenty of reasons, the number one being you."

She stepped into his arms and lifted her face for his kiss. The kiss was long, slow and deep.

When they came up for air, Bull pressed his forehead to hers, wishing they could spend the night there rather than at some boring event with a bunch of politicians. He'd rather spend the evening in her arms, holding her, loving her.

Layla leaned back and looked up into his eyes. "We'd better go."

She was right, and he knew it.

CHAPTER 8

BULL SIGHED, took Layla's hand and led her to the door and down to the embassy entrance. A line of cars awaited them.

Bull handed Layla into the middle SUV, her father followed, settling into the back seat. Bull claimed the front seat, and they were whisked away to the hotel where the event would take place with a lead vehicle and a trailing vehicle filled with the Ambassador's personal guards.

Bull's cellphone vibrated in his pocket and he pulled it out. "Farm animals en route." He grinned and tucked the cellphone back into his pocket. He was glad to know that his team would be there tonight. After that day's riot, he'd feel better knowing he had backup.

When they arrived at the hotel, Bull got out first

and looked around to make sure no danger existed before he helped Layla and her father out of the vehicle. He whisked Layla inside where they walked through the gauntlet of the reception line, which consisted of at least a dozen Turkish government officials to include Murat Akar, the Minister of Justice.

The man took Layla's hand and dipped his head briefly. "So glad you could be with us tonight," he said. "You are most beautiful."

She tipped her head and gave him a tight smile. "Thank you."

Bull looked around for Akar's sidekick from the other night and spotted Hasan Saka in the ballroom speaking with other men who appeared to be members of the Turkish government.

Something about Saka crept across Bull's skin in a bad way. He'd keep an eye on the man throughout the evening.

His gaze panned the room, searching for three familiar faces. Had the team arrived?

"Would you like to get a drink?" Layla asked.

"I could go for water or coffee," Bull said. No alcohol for him. He was there to protect Layla and needed a clear head to do that.

She hooked her hand through his elbow and led him to a table with crystal glasses and an urn of water with lemons floating among the ice cubes. She poured a glass for him and one for her and handed his to him. "To making it through the evening," she said and touched her glass to his.

"To making it back to the embassy early," he countered, his gaze locking with hers.

"Better," she said and took a sip while glancing around the room.

At that moment, a man in a black suit entered the ball room and tugged at the tie around his neck.

Bull fought the smile twitching at the corners of his lips.

Rucker looked about as uncomfortable as Bull had felt when he'd dressed for his first meeting with the US Ambassador to Turkey. He managed to avoid the reception line and crossed the room to take up a position at the opposite end.

Moments later, Mac entered, wearing a similar black suit with a navy blue tie. He, too, skipped the line and headed for the eastern side of the ballroom where he leaned his shoulder against a column, appearing not to care who passed.

Blade sailed through the entrance to the ballroom, wearing a black suit with a satin lapel. He smiled as he entered, his gaze panning the room before he found the reception line and introduced himself to every dignitary.

"What are you grinning about?" Layla asked.

Bull toned down his amusement at his teammate. "Nothing. Should we join your father? He looks like he could use some moral support."

Bull offered Layla his arm and marched her toward where her father stood.

The ambassador seemed to be having difficulties extricating himself from a conversation with a short, round man who walked alongside the US Ambassador, talking non-stop.

"Father," Layla touched the ambassador's arm, "there's someone I think you should meet." She smiled graciously at the man beside her father. "Pardon me. Could I steal my father away for a minute?"

"By all means." The man gave a slight bow and stepped away from the US Ambassador.

Layla gripped her father's elbow and led him toward the French and German Ambassadors who stood beside the bar, ordering glasses of wine.

"Comm check inside," Rucker's voice sounded in Bull's ear.

Bull turned and stepped a couple feet away from Layla and her father. "Bull, check."

Across the ballroom, Bull noticed Blade smiling and nodding to a woman who passed in front of him. Once she'd gone by, Blade's lips barely moved, but his voice came across clearly, "Blade, check."

From the far eastern corner of the room, Mac gave a slight nod. "Mac, check."

Rucker stood with his back to the wall, his face poker straight, his gaze on the people filling the ballroom. "Comm check outside."

"Dawg, check," Dawg's voice sounded in Bull's ear.

"Tank, check." The team medic's gravelly tone was unmistakable.

"Dash, check."

"Lance, check."

All eight men of the Delta Force team were accounted for.

"Perimeter status?" Rucker asked.

"Quiet," Dash reported. "Set up perimeter a block away to avoid the guards the Turks have on the building. We counted twelve. Four on the entrance alone."

"There's a steady line of vehicles dropping off more guests. Many of the dignitaries brought along their own bodyguards," Dawg added. "They're lurking near the entrance, making a crowd."

Thankfully, Layla and her father had arrived early enough to avoid the line. Still, Bull didn't like anything about the evening. With so many government officials and ambassadors from the many embassies, they made a convenient target for whatever rebel cause chose to make a violent statement.

Bull made a point to locate all the exits, noting the ones closest to Layla in case they had to bug out at any time during the evening. Mac, Rucker and Blade would help get them and Ambassador Grey out of the building as expeditiously as possible.

A string quartet played in a corner of the large

ballroom, but no one danced. People seemed content to mingle and exchange pleasantries with each other. Men wore either nice business suits or the military regalia of their position or country. Ladies displayed a variety of gowns and jewels, all appearing to be quite expensive.

Layla moved from group to group with her father, smiling and greeting each person individually, making each feel as important as the last. She introduced Bull as Mr. Smith, her fiancé. She always smiled at him when she did and reached for his hand, drawing him into the conversation.

A few minutes into these little group conversations, he'd ease out of the circle, more interested in keeping an eye on what was going on with the rest of the people in the room.

The large ballroom filled, making it more difficult to keep tabs on everyone. Bull became more tense as the night wore on and more people crowded into the space.

Layla and her father were talking with a group of Turkish government officials when the Minister of Justice, Murat Akar joined them. The group got into a lively discussion about a proposed bill that had the potential to impact human rights.

The head of the Interior Ministry argued with others, insisting it would guard against organizations taking root and raising money for terrorist attacks on the people of Turkey or neighboring countries.

Layla and her father stood by politely but didn't add to the heated discussion.

Bull leaned close to Layla. "Are all events this lively?"

She smiled up at him. "Some even more so. But for the most part, people maintain a polite façade. I imagine everyone is a little on edge since the demonstration this afternoon."

"How long are you required to stay here?" Bull asked.

"We usually stay until after the first government official leaves. That shouldn't be too much longer."

Bull nodded and glanced around the room. No one appeared to be leaving anytime soon. He tried to spot Mac, Blade and Rucker. With so many people crowded into the space, he couldn't locate his team.

They'd already been there for over an hour. Bull had begun to wish he was wearing his running shoes rather than the shiny black dress shoes he hadn't even had the chance to break in .

"Look," Layla said, tilting her head toward the entrance. "The Minister of the Interior is leaving."

Bull glanced toward the man walking out the door. "Does that mean we get to go?"

"Soon. I need to get my father to disengage." She stepped up to her father, who was in a discussion with the Minister of Justice. She waited for him to finish speaking before she addressed her father.

"Don't you have an early meeting tomorrow morning?" she said.

The ambassador took her hand. "I do. We won't stay much longer." He turned to Akar. "Please, pardon me. I believe it's time for me to leave."

He'd just turned away from Akar when several men dressed in the uniforms of the Turkish guards pushed through the crowd, knocking people over, their weapons pulled from their holsters.

Bull had only seconds to react.

He grabbed Layla and pulled her backward into his chest. "We need to get out of here. Nothing about this is right."

"Why do you say that?" she asked turning to see the guards heading toward them. "I wonder what's wrong."

THE UNIFORMED GUARDS appeared to be headed toward Layla and her father's group. They lifted their weapons, aiming in their direction.

Some guests shouted while others screamed, setting off a chain reaction of chaos as the crowd rushed for the front exit.

Bull pushed Layla to the ground and grabbed her father's arm. "Get down!"

Ambassador Grey dropped to his hands and knees and then flattened himself to the floor.

Gunfire blasted through the air.

Bull threw his body over Layla's.

More screaming sounded and there was a mad rush for the front door. People scrambled past them, some tripping over Bull and Layla where they lay.

The Minister of Justice crumpled to the floor beside them and lay still. He had a hole blasted through his pristine black suit and blood pooled across the shiny marble floor.

Layla gasped beneath Bull.

Still shielding her body, he looked up to see the guards turning to aim at another group of government officials pushing against the crowd to get out of the building.

"Bull?" Rucker's voice sounded in his ear.

"We're okay," he replied.

"Take the side exit," Rucker said. "Blade and I have it covered."

More shots were fired, this time from another direction.

While the armed men had their backs to Bull, Layla and the ambassador, they had to make their move.

Bull gripped Layla's arm and pulled her to her feet. He grabbed her father's elbow and helped him stand. "Stay low and move fast," he said and hurried them toward the nearest side exit, hoping they'd make it before the crowd discovered that this door was closer.

Rucker and Blade stood beside the door.

As Bull and his charges approached, Blade flung open the door. "The guys have you covered. Go!"

Bull wrapped his arm around Layla, shielding her body with his as they stepped out into the night.

"We're to head south for a couple blocks. Dash and the boys will pick us up once they can get back to the vehicles and circle the crowd," Rucker said.

"Mac?" Bull asked.

"Got out the opposite side. He's headed for the vehicles."

Bull didn't like that they were unarmed in a city that had become dangerous. The best he could do was to get the ambassador and his daughter as far away from the rogue guards as possible and back to the embassy compound.

He hoped the aggression was concentrated on the hotel and wouldn't spread throughout the city or target foreigners.

His team would have to assess the situation, once they arrived at the embassy. They just had to get to the embassy first.

CHAPTER 9

LAYLA DID the best she could in high heels and a dress, running between her father and Bull. She couldn't get the image of Akar lying on the floor beside her, his eyes open, staring straight at her as if accusing her of killing him.

Why had the Turkish guards turned on the government officials? Or were they really part of the Turkish military or just men dressed as guards?

A heavy weight settled low in her belly. Those men hadn't had to break into the hotel to mount their attack. They'd been inside all along. Layla would bet they'd been recruited by the resistance for just such an occasion. To assassinate members of the current administration.

When she was almost to the point she'd rather walk on glass barefooted than take another step in her high heeled shoes, Bull eased them to a stop at a corner.

Layla bent over to suck air into her starving lungs. By the time she straightened, two vehicles pulled to a halt in front of them and a guy got out, opened the door to the back seat and stood back.

Bull handed Layla into the seat while introducing the man holding the door. "Layla, this is Mac. Mac, Ms. Layla Grey and her father, Ambassador Grey."

Mac grinned and dipped his head. "Ms. Grey. Ambassador Grey. Glad to see you made it out of there in one piece."

Layla scooted to the middle, her father got in beside her, and Bull rounded the vehicle and got in on the other side of Layla. Mac took the front seat with the driver.

"Say hello to your driver, Dawg," Mac said.

Layla frowned. "Dawg?"

"Nickname," Dawg said with a grimace into the rearview mirror. "Don't ask. The guys can be real jerks."

Layla craned her neck to make sure the other two men had a ride.

Blade and Rucker had climbed into the second car. They sped away from the hotel.

Layla leaned back in the seat, willing her pulse to slow and her heart to stop pounding in her chest like a base drum. When she was more in control, she turned to Bull. "What just happened?"

"I'm not sure." Bull's jaw tightened. "Looked like the guards inside the hotel were anti-government and did their best to eliminate some of their current officials."

"But at a fundraiser for childhood cancer?" Layla shook her head. "What's happening is insane."

"Some people would consider it their only means to fight back against an oppressive dictatorship," Mac said from the front seat. "A dictatorship hiding behind a façade of a republic where the people actually have no say in what's going on."

"The president is pushing for another term, even though Turkey's constitution has term limits on the presidency," Bull said. "This president's term is up."

When they arrived at the embassy, Bull's team dropped off Bull, Layla and the ambassador at the gate and drove off. The guards were on high alert due to the shooting at the hotel. They thoroughly inspected their documentation and ran them through the scanners before they would allow them inside.

"I notified my security team that I'm back at the embassy," the ambassador said. "They'll bring back the vehicles when things calm down out there." He led the way into the embassy foyer. "Anybody up for a drink?"

Layla went to her father and gave him a big hug. "I'm sorry, Dad, but I'm beat. All I want to do is get out of these heels and go to bed."

He nodded. "I understand. I have to admit I was

shaken by that breach of security and the death of the Minister of Justice. The Turkish president will be furious and demand an investigation. I'm going to take a few minutes to report in to DC and the folks at Langley, and I'll be right behind you. I'm tired, too." The ambassador stuck out his hand to Bull. "Thank you and your team for getting us out of there."

Bull nodded. "I'm just glad we were able to, and that you had the foresight to deploy the entire team to the event. We couldn't have done it without all of us."

The ambassador nodded. "And thank you for making sure my daughter didn't get caught in the crossfire."

"Or you, Daddy," Layla said.

Bull held out his hand, Layla placed hers in his and they walked to the elevator. Once inside and the doors had closed, she stepped into his arms.

"Thank you," she said, "That could have been me lying on the floor instead of the Minister of Justice."

He hugged her close. "I think I lost ten years off my life in that two or three seconds."

The elevator dinged, and the door slid open.

Layla laughed. "We got our wish of getting out of there early."

"I would have preferred a different reason," Bull said.

"But now that we're here and we're safe..." she

said and leaned into him as they walked down the hallway, "the night does not have to end."

They paused in front of her quarters while she fished her key out of the hidden pocket in her dress. She unlocked the door and pushed it open. Before she could take a step inside, he scooped her up in his arms and carried her across the threshold.

Yes, she could have walked, but being held in a strong man's arms was so much better. And the promise of what was to come left her shivering with anticipation.

When he set her back on her feet, he held her close and kissed her.

Layla leaned up on her toes and opened to him, letting their tongues intertwine. Heat built at her center and spread from her core outward. She wanted the kiss to go on forever.

Alas, they had to breathe.

Layla rested her cheek on his chest, listening to the thundering beat of his heart. "I think I needed that."

He tipped her head up and kissed her forehead. "I need a whole lot more than that."

She smiled and pushed his jacket off his shoulders.

He yanked the necktie from around his neck and tossed it to the corner of the room.

Layla started working loose the buttons of his shirt, one at a time. She pulled the tails of his shirt from the waistband of his trousers and ran her hands across his bare chest.

He kissed her on the lips again, and then stepped back, spun her around and dragged the tab of her zipper slowly down her back. Then he pushed the straps from her shoulders.

The dress slipped from her body and pooled at her feet. All she wore beneath it was a pair of silky thong panties and her high heels.

His gaze swept over her, making her feel deliciously sexy. He knelt beside her, loosened the buckles of her shoes and slipped them from her feet. Then he hooked his thumbs in the elastic of her panties, dragged them down to her ankles and helped her step free.

"I've been waiting for this all night," he said, "And it is so worth the wait."

She didn't feel embarrassed about standing naked in front of him. In fact, she felt desire washing over her. She ran her hands from her hips up her torso to cup her own breasts. The nipples had already tightened into tight little buds. "Aren't you overdressed, soldier?"

He moaned. "Yes, ma'am."

Layla smoothed her hands beneath his shirt and started to push the garment over his shoulders.

A knock sounded at the door. Her hands froze.

Bull glanced toward the door. "Want me to answer it?"

Layla shook her head. "No. Let's wait a minute and see if they'll go away."

Bull and Layla stood frozen where they had started and waited.

Layla prayed that whoever was at the door would just give up and go away.

Another knock sounded, this one a little more urgent.

"Ms. Grey, Mr. Smith," Pinar's voice sounded on the other side of the door. "If you're in there I have need of you."

Bull pulled his shirt back over his shoulders and secured a few buttons. "I'll get this."

Before he went to the door though he scooped her up, laid her in the bed, and covered her with the sheet. "Hold that thought," he said.

She circled her hand behind his neck and pulled him down for a quick kiss. "Don't be long."

He turned and hurried toward the door, opened it and looked down at the personal assistant. "Yes, ma'am?"

She grabbed his arm. "I need you downstairs immediately."

"What's wrong?" he asked.

Layla clutched the sheet to her chest and craned her neck to see around Bull.

"It's Ambassador Grey. He's got himself locked in the downstairs bathroom. He needs assistance getting out."

Layla chuckled. The bathroom outside his study had a tricky doorknob that occasionally got stuck. If wiggled enough, whoever was locked inside was usually able to get out. Until now.

Bull sighed. "Don't you have a maintenance person who could help him out?"

She shook her head. "They've all gone home for the evening. They won't be back until the morning."

He glanced over his shoulder at Layla.

She hid a grin.

"I'll be back in a few minutes," he said, with a grimace. "Don't go anywhere."

She raised a hand. "Believe me, I'm not going anywhere."

He left the room, pulling the door closed behind him. Layla lay back against the pillows, a smile on her face. The night promised to be magic, and Bull was the magician. She laughed at her thoughts. She really liked the man. She could be falling in love with him. Her smile faded, and she was back to the dilemma of him being a Delta, and she was the ambassador's daughter. Her cellphone buzzed on the charger on the nightstand, indicating an incoming text message.

She leaned over, letting the sheet slide down from her bare breasts. Soon, Bull's hand would be sliding over her breasts. Maybe he was texting her from downstairs. She picked up the phone and stared down at the text message. It wasn't Bull. It was Miriam Rogers.

Miriam: Cover is blown. You won't hear from us. We're going deep. Clean your phone and keep your head low. If I need to contact you, I'll send a message by courier.

Layla: Be safe, my friend

Layla's hand tightened on her cellphone, as cold dread filled her chest. Miriam and her network of angels were in trouble. She had been very careful not to reveal Layla's true identity to the rest of the network. Miriam was the only one who knew that she was the ambassador's daughter. But if Miriam was compromised, whoever had blown their cover could lead them back to Layla and the US embassy.

She swung her legs out of the bed, pulled a T-shirt out of her drawer, slipped it over her head, and pulled on a pair of jeans. Her hands shook as she buttoned the top button. Yes, she wanted to help people, and she was proud of what she'd done for the women that they'd rescued. But now, she could be in trouble, and if she was in trouble, that could compromise her father's position as ambassador.

Layla paced the room. What should she do? She wanted to run out into the street, find Miriam and keep her safe, but Miriam had said she was going deep. She might even have to leave the country. Hell, Layla might have to leave the country.

She slipped on a pair of socks and tennis shoes and gave a shaky laugh at herself. What was she going to do, run out the door and keep running until she left Turkey? She hated that the underground railroad had been exposed and wondered who had violated their trust. Now, there wouldn't be anybody out there to help the women who were being traded and sold like cattle.

When a knock came at her door, she almost cried out in relief. Finally, Bull was back. Maybe he could help her figure out what she should do next. Her father might get his wish; she might have to go back to the States sooner rather than later. Maybe he'd task Bull to make sure she got there safely. She ran to the door and yanked it open.

Her personal assistant stood there.

Layla frowned. "Where's Bull?"

The woman gave a small smile. "He's still working on getting that door open for your father."

"Do you need my help?" Layla started through the door.

Pinar held up her hand and shook her head. "No. I think he has everything under control."

"Then why are you here?"

Pinar pulled an envelope from her pocket and handed it to her. "This came for you. It was left at the gate. The guard brought it inside. I thought you might need it." She handed her the envelope. "I'll get back downstairs and see what I can do to help your father." Pinar left Layla in her doorway.

She closed the door and ripped open the envelope. The message was cryptic.

Need your help. Meet me behind the coffee shop. Come alone.

M.R.

Layla stared at the words on the page. Miriam was in trouble and needed Layla's help. She didn't like the idea of going out alone. Not after all that had happened over the last two days. Not since Bull had provided her protection. But she couldn't leave her friend out there alone. Not when she needed help. The woman had helped so many others.

Layla had to do something. But what if she was captured? No one would know where to look for her. It wasn't like she was carrying some hidden GPS device. Then she remembered her cellphone and her watch. Both had tracking apps on them. She slipped her watch onto her wrist and shoved her cellphone into the back pocket of her jeans. Pulling on a hooded jacket, she tucked her hair inside it.

Layla pulled a sheet of stationery out of her night-stand, scribbled a note for Bull, folded it and laid it on the pillow. She had given him a key to get into the room. When he returned, he'd find it empty, and then he'd find the note and know where she'd gone, and that she was wearing her watch and carrying her cellphone. Her lips curled into a smile. She'd signed the note, *I think I love you, Layla.*

Finally ready, she slipped out of her room, ran down the hall and took the stairs to the level where the library was. The hidden doorway opened easily, and the lights lit up in the tunnel. Layla hurried through it. When she reached the outside door, she paused and peered out. The street was empty and dark. The coffee shop where she'd originally met Miriam was a couple blocks walk to the west. She turned left and started out at a good pace.

Headlights blinked on a car that was sitting on the side of the road. Layla's heart stuttered, and a ripple of fear snaked its way down her spine. The car was in front of her. She spun on her heel and walked away from it as fast as she could. The car's engine revved, and the headlights seemed to be moving closer.

Layla walked faster. The vehicle was quickly approaching. Instead of speeding up and going past her, it slowed. Layla gave up all pretense of walking and ran. She couldn't go back to the hidden door and lead whoever was following her back into the embassy. She ran past it searching for an alleyway, a street, anything she could turn down to escape the oncoming car, but she couldn't run fast enough.

The vehicle caught up with her, went just a little bit past her and two men leaped out.

Layla turned and ran the other direction as fast as she could. Again, she wasn't fast enough. The two men gained on her, their footsteps pounding the pavement behind her. She could scream, but she was on the backside of the embassy, far away from any of the guards who might hear her.

One of the men grabbed the back of her jacket.

She let him have it. He ripped it from her arms as she kept running. Layla didn't get far before the other one tackled her. She crashed to the ground, her head bouncing off the pavement.

Pain stabbed through her forehead, the street-lights dimmed, and she lost consciousness.

CHAPTER 10

WHAT SHOULD HAVE TAKEN ONLY five minutes, ended up taking ten. Bull had spent the better part of that time looking for tools to disassemble the lock on the bathroom door.

The ambassador tried to be helpful by telling him where the tools could be located. It would've been a lot faster if he'd have just kicked the door in, but the door was one of those heavy kinds, solid wood and old. He figured the doorjamb was probably just as solid as the wood of the door. After a few cuss words, scraping his knuckles at least twice, and more or less dismantling the handle on the door, he got it open.

"Thank you, son," the ambassador said, "I've had a work order out on that lock for at least two weeks. Until they get it fixed, I'll have them put up a sign that this restroom is out of service."

"That would be a good idea, sir," Bull said, anxious to get back to his fiancée. "Now if you'll excuse me..."

"Thank you for rescuing me yet again tonight," the ambassador said. "You don't know how much it means to me that you're taking care of my daughter."

A stab of guilt hit Bull square in the gut. Hopefully, the ambassador didn't know the extent to which he was *taking care* of his daughter. He really didn't want to stand around talking when he could be upstairs attending to her.

"Sir, it's my pleasure," and that was an understatement. The ambassador didn't need to know just how much of an understatement it was.

"I need to send my daughter back to the States. She should have a life of her own apart from me. I'd get along fine without her. Granted, I'd be a little lonely. But I don't want her to miss out on what I had with her mother. She deserves the chance to find somebody, fall in love and have a family and children of her own." The ambassador smiled. "After all, I want grandchildren."

"She'd make a good mother," Bull said. "I got to see her in action with the orphans. They loved her." And Bull had found himself loving her as well. She was everything he could ever want in a woman. Beautiful, compassionate, understanding.

Still, it wouldn't be fair to her if she gave up her life with her father to be with him. He was Delta Force.

Deltas were never home. If they had children together, Layla would raise them alone. He'd miss every birthday party. He'd miss her birthdays. More often than not, he wouldn't be home for anniversaries or Christmas. He wouldn't be there to fix the pipes when they broke or to mow the lawn. She'd have to carry the burden for both of them, and that wasn't fair.

"She would do well to marry a man like you," the ambassador said.

Bull shook his head. "Sir, I'm Delta Force. I wouldn't wish that on any woman."

The older man clapped his hand on his shoulder. "Don't sell yourself short. If a woman loves you enough and understands the nature of your work, she'd be willing to wait for you and be there to welcome you with open arms. You're a good man, Bull. If anything were to develop between you and my daughter, you'd have my blessing."

His heart squeezed tightly at the man's words. "Thank you, Ambassador Grey. Now, if you'd excuse me, I'd like to get back to her. I've left her alone long enough."

The ambassador nodded. "By all means."

He hurried to the elevator and up to the floor where Layla would be waiting in her quarters. His feet carried him faster. The thought of Layla lying in the bed naked had his groin tightening in anticipation. He slid the key in, turned the knob and stepped inside, closing the door behind him. When he faced the room, he frowned. The bed was empty.

"Layla," he called out. No response. He pushed open the door to the bathroom. It too was empty. A bad feeling pinched his chest. Where would she have gone without him? He glanced at her nightstand where she kept her cellphone.

It was gone.

He crossed to the bed and felt the sheets. They were still warm. She hadn't been gone long.

Then he noticed the note on the pillow. He unfolded it and read, his heart sinking to his knees.

Dear Mr. Smith, I'm off to see a friend in trouble. I have to do this alone. If I'm not back in fifteen minutes, I'll have my cellphone and my watch with me.

I think I love you, Layla

Bull's heart squeezed so hard in his chest, he couldn't breathe. She'd left without him, and he didn't know where to go look. He read the note again, pulled out his cellphone and dialed hers. It rang at least seven times before it went to her voicemail. Why wasn't she answering? And why had she mentioned her watch? She wouldn't have mentioned those if she didn't have a reason.

And then he thought, perhaps she had a tracker on her phone. He grabbed his radio headset, stuck the earbuds in his ears and ran for the elevator.

On the way down in the elevator, he texted Rucker.

Bull: Have a situation here.

Rucker: Need the team?

Bull: Yes. Be on standby.

He had to get to the ambassador before he went to bed. Bull had no idea where the man slept.

The elevator door opened.

The ambassador stood there, waiting to step in. "Did you forget something, Mr. Smith?"

"Ambassador Grey, do you have a tracking app on your phone for your daughter's phone?"

He frowned. "I believe I do. She put an app on my phone so that she could keep track of me, and she said that I could use it to keep track of her." He grimaced. "If I could just get her to carry her phone. But I think it will also track her watch."

"Sir, I need your phone and that app. Now."

Ambassador Grey frowned. "What's the problem? Where's my daughter?"

"That seems to be the question. When I got back to her room, she was gone. She'd left a note that said she was going out to help a friend."

The older man's frown deepened. "What friend?"

"I think I have an idea of who that might be," Bull said, "but I need that app."

"I left my phone in the study, follow me." The ambassador led the way to his study. His phone was on his desk on the charger. He unlocked the screen, clicked on an app, and handed it over to Bull.

When he glanced down at the map, Bull's gut clenched.

The ambassador leaned over his shoulder. "Her phone shows that she's right outside of the back of the embassy."

"I know where that is. Come with me," Bull said. He grabbed the ambassador's arm, pulled him into the elevator and went up to the floor where the library was located. He led him to the back wall of the library and pulled the sconce. The bookshelf door opened.

"So, this is where it is," the ambassador said. "I'd heard there was a secret passage in the building, but no one seemed to know where it was or how to access it. You think my daughter went through here?"

Bull nodded. "I'd bet my annual pay she did." He led the way through the narrow passage, down the stairs, through the tunnel and out onto the street. Using the ambassador's phone, he followed the GPS tracking on it.

Bull squinted into the darkness. "This shows that she should be just right up the street." The street appeared empty.

"I don't see her," the ambassador said.

Bull ran to the spot the GPS indicated. Layla was nowhere in sight. He dialed her number again and heard the ringing of a cellphone. He followed the sound and found her phone lying face down on the ground. He lifted it and turned it over. The screen was cracked as if it had fallen or been thrown.

"Oh, baby," the ambassador said. "Where are you?"

Bull's cellphone buzzed with an incoming text. He glanced down, hoping it would be Layla, texting from someone else's phone. It was Rucker.

Rucker: We're on standby, what's happening?

Bull glanced at the locater app on the ambassador's phone.

"You should be able to see where her watch is as well," the ambassador said.

He looked at the screen, studied it closely, then enlarged it so he could see it better in the dark. The watch was moving, headed toward the edge of the city.

Bull called Rucker on his cellphone. "Pick me up in front of the embassy as soon as possible."

"What's going on?" Rucker asked.

A hollow feeling settled in Bull's chest. "Ms. Grey is gone."

"What do you mean, she's gone?" Rucker asked. "I thought you were keeping an eye on her."

Bull was still kicking himself. He should've had her come with him when he went to help her father get out of the bathroom. He shouldn't have left her for even a second. Never mind the door was locked to her bedroom, and they were supposedly secure inside the embassy. The woman hadn't been taken. She'd left of her own free will.

The very reason why he loved her was also the reason she was now missing. She was too empathetic and compassionate. She responded when other people needed her, even if it put her in danger. And he suspected, right now, that she was in danger. If she had gone because a friend was in trouble, then she was putting herself in the same amount of trouble. And the rate that she was moving toward the edge of the city, it wouldn't be long before they left Ankara altogether.

"I have a way to track her," he told Rucker, "but I need wheels. Can you get here soon?"

"On our way now."

Bull turned to the ambassador. "Ambassador Grey, I know you'll want to come with me, but I think it would be best if you stay here at the embassy in case she returns before I get back."

"But she's my daughter," he said, "I want to be there."

"Sir, you'll only slow us down." He squared off with the ambassador. "Sir, if she's helping who I think she is, and you're caught with that person, it could compromise your duties here as the ambassador."

The man's eyes narrowed. "What exactly is my daughter up to?"

"I'll have her explain it when we get back. Right now, I need to get you inside where you're safe. And we need to put a guard on this escape tunnel."

The ambassador hurried back with Bull through the secret tunnel and into the embassy. Bull left the diplomat in his study and walked out the front entrance of the embassy as Rucker and the team pulled to a stop in the two vehicles they had rented.

Bull climbed into the front passenger side of the lead vehicle, gave them directions toward the edge of the city and leaned forward in his seat as if that would get him there faster. While Rucker drove, Bull filled them in on what Layla had been involved in.

When he was done Rucker whistled. "Sex trafficking is big business," he said. "Sounds like this underground network has really cut into that. The mafia handling it has to be really pissed off."

"That's what I'm afraid of, and if they get a hold of Layla there's no telling what they'll do with her."

Rucker shook his head. "We can hope that they just want to ransom her, and that they'll keep her alive and healthy until they get what they demand."

"We don't even know if they have her," Bull said. "She could be with her contact, and I could be worried for nothing."

Rucker shot a glance his direction. "And what does your gut tell you?"

His gut was knotted. "It tells me that she's in big trouble, and she's headed out of the city but not on her own steam."

"Why did she leave without you in the first place?" Rucker asked.

"She knows I don't approve of her actions, but mostly, I wasn't with her when she got whatever communication from her friend. I was helping her father. I'd left her in her room for just a few minutes, and that's all it took. Now, she's gone." Bull shook his head. "I shouldn't have left her."

Rucker shot another glance his direction. "You like her, don't you?"

Bull nodded. "More than I should."

Blade leaned over the back of the seat. "What's not to like? She was a knockout in that dress tonight."

Bull glared back at Blade. "It's not all about the looks."

"Maybe not," Blade said with a grin, "but it helps."

"She really cares about her family, about her friends and people who aren't as fortunate as she is. She helps the orphans, and she wanted to help the women who were being trafficked. She has a good heart."

Rucker chuckled. "You're falling for her."

"I can't," Bull said. "I'm a Delta."

Rucker laughed. "Even Deltas can fall in love. I mean, look at me. I did with someone who knew exactly what kind of job I had, understood it and could deal with it. Nora is the best thing that could ever have happened to me. She gets me."

"And look at Dash," Blade said. "That lucky bastard landed Sunny Day. And those two are so in love, it almost makes my teeth hurt."

Bull glanced across at Rucker. "But do you think it'll last?"

Rucker nodded. "Relationships are like anything worthwhile, you have to work at it."

"And how do you do that," Bull said, "when you're deployed nearly three-hundred and sixty-five days a year?"

Rucker shook his head. "We're not deployed that often. You just have to make up for it with the time you have together. And she has to be strong enough to manage on her own when you're not there. Sounds to me like Ms. Grey is a strong-minded woman. She didn't fall apart during the demonstration this afternoon nor during the shooting this evening."

Bull smiled. "And you should've seen her getting Yara out of her situation. She didn't hesitate. She jumped right in."

"That's the kind of woman a Delta needs," Rucker said.

Blade leaned forward again. "So, does this Layla have a sister?"

"No," Bull said, "and if she did, I sure as hell wouldn't introduce her to you."

Blade sat back. "That's cold, brother. That's cold."

"Where are they now?" Rucker asked.

"They appear to be headed east into the mountains. No, wait, I think they've stopped on the edge of the city."

Rucker slowed at the corner and sped up after the turn. "How far are we from them?"

"I can only guess, maybe eight, ten miles," Bull said.

"Moving through city streets, that could take us anywhere from fifteen to thirty minutes."

"I hope we get there soon enough," Bull said.

"Me, too." Rucker pressed his foot harder to the accelerator, moving as quickly as he could through the streets.

Bull alternated between staring at the phone app and the road ahead. He prayed that Layla was okay, and that they reached her in time.

CHAPTER 11

LAYLA AWOKE IN COMPLETE DARKNESS, her body cramped into a tight space. The rumbling and vibration beneath her cheek and the hard metal above her quickly made it clear to her that she was in the trunk of a vehicle. She could tell when it slowed, and when it sped up. Based on the number of times they did, and the turns they made, she could only guess that they were still somewhere in the city. She had no idea how long she'd been out.

Trapped in a trunk, her only saving grace was that her captors hadn't taken the time to tie her up. She couldn't open the trunk from inside, so she'd have to wait until they opened the trunk to get her out. At that point, she'd have to make a break for it. Before they tied her up.

Seconds passed into minutes, minutes passed into...how long, she didn't know. The longer they drove, the farther away they took her from Bull, the embassy and her father. She felt in her back pocket for her phone. It was gone. Thankfully, they hadn't removed her watch from her wrist. Not only did her watch have a tracking device on it, but she could also make calls from it if she had enough of a signal. Whatever she did she had to conserve the battery on the watch. It was the only way Bull and his team could find her. It had to stay on. She raised the phone to her mouth and spoke quietly.

"Call Bull."

She waited while it connected and held the device up to her ear.

It rang once, and Bull's voice came over on the line. "Layla, are you all right?"

She pressed a hand to the tender spot on her forehead. "Other than a bump on my head, I'm okay."

"I found your phone," he said. "I assume that you're not traveling on your free will."

"No," she said, "I'm not. I need to keep this brief so that I can conserve my battery."

"We're coming for you. We're following you on your father's phone app."

She smiled. "Thank God," she said.

"What's your situation?"

"I'm pretty sure I'm in the trunk of a car. I don't know where we're heading. All I know about my captors is that two guys got out of the car that tried to run me down. At least one other had to be driving.

I'm not sure why they grabbed me or what their intentions are."

"Can you breathe?"

The inside of the trunk smelled of tire rubber and dust, but there was enough air to sustain her for a while. "I can breathe."

"We're ten to fifteen minutes behind you."

She gulped. "Okay. Could you improve that time a little?"

"We'll do the best we can," he said. "Don't worry. We're coming."

The car was slowing, and it came to a stop. "Gotta go, they're stopping."

"Hang in there, sweetheart. I think I love you, too."

Her heart fluttered at his words. He might just be saying them because she'd included them in her note. But hearing him say he thought he loved her made hope swell inside her, giving her the strength she needed to attempt an escape.

Ten to fifteen minutes wasn't terrible, but she didn't really know how long she had before the people who had her decided what they wanted to do with her. Ten to fifteen minutes might be the differ-ence between life and death, depending on what these guys had in mind. But then, wouldn't they have killed her if they wanted her dead? Why load her alive in the back of a vehicle unless they wanted her to stay alive?

When the vehicle came to a full stop, she could feel it shift into park. Doors creaked open and slammed closed.

Layla bunched her muscles. She tried to get into a position where she could jump out, but it was hard when she was lying on her side. She got ready to roll over onto her feet.

The lid popped up, and she sprang.

Two men were there. They grabbed her arms and pulled her out of the trunk. She fought, kicking and screaming, but they held fast. A big man wearing an overcoat stepped up to her and slapped her hard in the face. It made her head spin, and she almost lost consciousness again. When she blinked, the gray haze around her eyes receded. She looked into the face of a man she recognized.

Hasan Saka.

"I should have known it was you." She remembered seeing him at the hotel after the shots were fired. When the shit had hit the fan inside the ballroom, this man had stepped to the side and hugged a wall observing, not rushing out like everyone else. As if he had no fear of the men wielding the guns.

His lip turned up in a sneer. "What do you know, woman?"

"You staged the attack on the hotel," she guessed. "Those shooters worked for you."

His lip lifted in a sneer. "No one will ever know."

A cold chill rippled across Layla's skin. *No one will*

ever know meant he intended to make sure she never spilled the beans. He intended to kill her. But, if that was the case, why hadn't he done it already?

"What do you want with me?" Layla demanded.

He lifted his chin, glancing past her. "You will see soon enough."

Headlights appeared at the end of the street, and a car pulled to a stop. A person stepped out and stood behind the open car door.

"I'm here to make the trade." Miriam Rogers's voice sounded loud and clear.

A lead weight settled in the pit of Layla's belly. They were using her to get to Miriam. The note had been a setup.

Had Pinar Erim been in on it?

"Send the woman over," Miriam said.

Saka shook his head. "You will meet halfway."

"No way," Miriam said. "You'll kill us both."

That had to be what he intended. Layla couldn't let that happen. "Don't do it!" she called out. "Don't make the trade! Leave. Get away from here. Be safe."

Saka backhanded her with his fist, busting her lip.

Blood trickled across her chin. Layla wiped it away. It was nothing compared to the bloodshed this monster had in mind. "Don't do it! Save yourself," she said. "He isn't interested in a trade. He's gonna kill us both."

"Even if you leave without her, you won't get far," Saka said. "We know who you are, Miriam Rogers.

There's a price on your head, and I intend to collect it, dead or alive."

"You know you're going to be found out, don't you?" Layla said.

"Shut up, woman." He raised his hand to hit her again.

She turned her head in anticipation of the blow. "Those guards will talk. They will tell who gave them the orders to kill the Minister of Justice. They won't take the fall for you."

His hand paused, and his eyes narrowed. "You don't know that."

"And when they do let the president know who was responsible for the shooting at the gala, you won't be safe inside of Turkey. You don't need her," Layla said. Tipping her head toward Miriam Rogers. "You need me. Alive." It was a risk, but one she was willing to take.

He shot a glance her way, and his eyes narrowed. "What do you mean?"

"I'm the US Ambassador's daughter. I could be your ticket out of Turkey. All you have to do is hold me for ransom and ask for anything. Money, a helicopter, a plane to get out of here. What will Miriam Rogers buy you?"

His brow descended. "She stole from me."

Layla had to bite her tongue to keep from telling the man what she thought of him. "The women you planned to sell into the sex trade?"

"Their father's negotiated arranged marriages for them."

"Let me get that straight. They sold you those women—their daughters—for you to sell into arranged marriages?" She snorted. "And they believed you?" She shook her head. "Arranged marriages or brothels, I don't see much of a difference. Those women—those girls—would have led a life that wasn't worth living. They aren't animals to be sold or traded. They're human beings with thoughts and feelings. They feel pain and sadness."

"I bought them. I paid money for them. My clients paid me for a product I could not deliver."

"Women and children are not products to be bought and sold. Is that why you killed the Minister of Justice? Had he got tired of turning a blind eye to your operation? Or did you owe him some of those women that you had purchased, and he threatened to out you to the president?"

"He talked too much, and you talk too much."

"What's it to be?" Miriam called out. "Send her over. You can have me for her."

"No trade is necessary," he said. "I will have you both."

Layla gasped. "You don't need her."

He laughed.

"You need to get out of Turkey. Your life is in danger here. You killed a government official. The president will not look kindly on that." Layla spoke fast, hoping to change the man's mind.

"He is a fool," Saka said. "He does not control his ministry. They do as they please. They are even more corrupt than he is."

Layla snorted. "More corrupt than you?"

Saka raised a hand, moving his finger in a circular motion. Men appeared out of the shadows and converged on Miriam's vehicle. She tried to jump back inside, but they caught her before she could leave or lock herself in. They yanked open the door and dragged her out in front of the headlights.

"Don't hurt her," Layla cried.

Saka smiled, a horrible, evil smile. "Why would I hurt her? She's worth money. She has a price on her head. I plan on cashing in on that price as well as ransoming you to buy my way out of Turkey. And I will have my revenge. I'm not the only businessman she has stolen from. She will not last long in jail. And once I ransom you, you and your father will be deported from Turkey for your connection with this woman."

Layla's heart sank as they dragged Miriam toward her.

"Take them inside and tie them up," he said in Turkish.

The two men holding Layla half-dragged, half-carried her into a warehouse behind them. Once inside, they used duct tape to bind her ankles and wrists. They did the same to Miriam and sat them both on the cold concrete floor several feet apart.

Hasan strode in and handed her a burner phone. "Call your father. Tell him he will come with two million dollars and a helicopter to get me out of here. And tell him to contact the Turkish president and inform him that he can have the terrorist Miriam Rogers for the price of the bounty on her head."

He shoved the phone into her hands. She struggled to punch the buttons for the number because of the bindings around her wrists, but she dialed her father's number and waited for it to ring.

"ARE WE GETTING CLOSE YET?" Rucker asked.

Bull held the cellphone in his grip, his body tense. "Two miles."

"We should slow down and look for a place to stop. We need to go in on foot," Rucker said.

Bull clenched his teeth. He knew Rucker was right, but he wanted to get there as fast as he could.

"We don't know how many people we're up against," Rucker reasoned. "It won't do Layla any good if we go blowing in there and are immediately surrounded, outmanned and outgunned. We need to have a clear idea of what's there."

Bull nodded. "You're right. Park it, and let's get in there."

When they were a mile and a half away from the indicated location, Rucker pulled into an alley.

The vehicle behind him parked beside them. All of the men piled out, performed a quick comm check, and then pulled their weapons out of the trunk.

"Thought you might like to have these." Rucker handed an additional M4A1 rifle, a Glock 9MM pistol and a holster to Bull.

The weight of the weapons in his hands felt good. When the team was ready, Bull nodded. "Let's go."

The men spread out and moved toward the location several blocks away with Bull on point. They clung to the shadows of the buildings around them, checking for bogies before stepping out into the open. When they were just a block away, Bull raised his fist, indicating they should stop. He spent a long moment studying the street and buildings ahead.

A movement in the shadows caught his attention. "Armed bogey, two o'clock."

From his position at the opposite corner, Rucker reported, "Another bogey, eleven o'clock."

The men carried AK-47 Russian-made rifles and appeared to be alert and watching.

"I'll take eleven," Rucker said.

"I've got two," Mac chimed in.

The Deltas made their move, slipping silently through the street, their guns slung across their backs, knives in their hands.

Another silhouette emerged from a shadow directly ahead of Bull. "Got another bogey, twelve o'clock. I'll take him," Bull said. He moved swiftly and silently, shadow to shadow, sneaking up on the man.

"Eleven neutralized," Rucker reported.

Bull hadn't heard a thing. No cries for help. No screams of terror. Just silence. His bogey struck a match and lit a cigarette. As the man concentrated on the flame at the end of his smoke, Bull made his move. He slipped in, grabbed the man behind the neck, and dispatched him with a single stroke. The cigarette and match fell to the ground, the flame burning out.

Bull dragged the man to the corner of an alley and dropped him in the shadows. "Twelve o'clock neutralized."

"Two o'clock neutralized," Mac reported.

Dash took point, having taken the lead as the other three took care of the perimeter guards. The team moved forward and spread out around the front of a warehouse building.

"Blade, Dawg, Lance, check the rear of the building. See if there are other entrances," Rucker ordered.

"Roger," all three men said at once.

The men moved out, circling wide around the warehouse.

Bull rocked forward, wanting to rush in, find Layla and get her the hell out.

"Steady, Bull," Rucker said. "Let the team report."

"Another bogey at the rear," Blade reported. "Got him. There's one door and its locked."

"What's the plan?" Bull asked. "They could be torturing her as we speak."

"Or they could shoot her as we blow through the doors," Rucker whispered. "Blade, did you bring what it takes to make a little noise?"

"Affirmative," Blade responded.

"Rig it, and let us know when you're ready," Rucker said.

"Roger."

"Dash and Mac, you guys take the guards on the front door." Rucker waved the two men forward. "Bull and I will breach."

"I'll take point," Bull said.

"Roger," Rucker said. "I'll cover."

Mac and Dash hugged the shadows until they reached the sides of the building, then moved along the front so quietly that the guards didn't see them until they were right on them. One of the guards called out before he was dispatched.

Bull cringed. The man's shouts could have warned those in the warehouse of the threat outside.

"Could use that noise right now," Rucker said.

"Ready," Blade responded. "Clear."

Bull waited for his cue—the sound of an explosion—to breach the doorway.

CHAPTER 12

WHILE THE GUARDS weren't looking, Layla tore into the duct tape with her teeth, ripping at it as fast as she could. Beside her, she could hear the telltale sounds of Miriam doing the same.

Hasan Saka stood several feet away, his cellphone pressed to his ear. She heard him speaking in Turkish.

Thankfully, it was dark enough in the warehouse that even if the guards had looked back to see what they were doing, they wouldn't have been able to make out the fact that they were tearing at their bonds. They would have to be a whole lot closer. And then something Saka said made her stop. Though she could only pick up a few words, she recognized him addressing the person he was talking to as "Mr. President."

Was he talking directly to the Turkish president?

Still tearing at the tape, she perked up her ears and scooted a little closer so that she could hear him better. From the gist of his conversation, it sounded more like he'd staged the attack on the Minister of Justice based on the president's orders. He added that the two women knew. Then she heard him say something that chilled her to the bones. He would take care of them. No one would ever know that the president was involved in the attack on the hotel.

Layla could forget negotiating for their lives in exchange for collecting the ransom from Layla's father or a bounty on Miriam Rogers.

Hasan Saka had just been ordered to kill them.

"Did you get that?" she whispered to Miriam.

"Yes," she whispered back. "We could sure use a miracle about now."

Hasan Saka ended his call, slowly turned toward the ladies on the floor and pulled a handgun from his pocket. He aimed from Layla to Miriam and hesitated. "Who first?"

"It appears to me," Layla said, desperate to buy time, "that you need a hostage, maybe two. One hostage the American people can get behind—the daughter of an American ambassador. The other being a freedom rider like Miriam Rogers. You need us, and you need the backing of the United States. Otherwise, you're taking the fall for the president, and once he implicates you in what happened at the hotel, he'll have no need for you and he'll tie up loose ends. That would be you. Which leads us back to the fact that you need to get out of the country, and we're your ticket."

He shook his head. "You and I both know the United States does not negotiate with terrorists. They would label me as a terrorist. I have my own way of getting out of the country. So, back to the question, who first? The one who stole my money?" He pointed the gun at Miriam. "Or she who talks too much?" He leveled the barrel of his weapon at Layla and narrowed his eyes. His finger moved off the trigger guard onto the trigger.

A shout from outside the warehouse made Saka turn.

Layla tore the last threads of the duct tape loose from her wrists. She had to get away, but her ankles were still bound.

Hasan Saka told one of the guards on the inside to go check and see what the noise was all about. Layla reached for the duct tape around her ankles and ripped it away as fast as she could.

The noise made Hasan turn toward her. He muttered a curse beneath his breath and raised his weapon again. Still bound at the ankles, Layla rolled to the side. Hasan fired his weapon at the same time a loud bang sounded from the backside of the warehouse.

The bullet hit somewhere close to where Layla had been moments before, missing her by inches.

The guards inside the warehouse shouted. Some started to run toward the rear to see what the noise was about. Hasan yelled at them.

They changed directions and ran toward a large van parked inside the warehouse.

Hasan Saka ran toward the van, yelling at one of the guards in Turkish. "Kill them! Kill them!"

The guard stood in the middle of the warehouse, looking between the women on the floor and the van being loaded with the other guards and Hasan, as if he couldn't decide whether he wanted to do as he was told or bail on the situation and get the hell out of there.

The front door to the warehouse blew open, and men carrying rifles stormed in.

The guard raced toward the van. Before he reached it, the van took off racing toward the men who'd just entered the warehouse. The men carrying the guns turned and aimed at the van barreling toward them.

"Don't shoot at the van!" someone yelled. "She might be in it."

Layla knew that voice, and she almost sobbed with relief. It was Bull, and the men were his team. The cavalry had arrived.

"Bull!" Layla called out. "We're not in that van. We're here."

The Deltas scattered out of the path of the oncoming vehicle.

The van crashed through the metal overhead door and burst out into the open.

The guard who'd missed the van swung his rifle toward the Deltas.

Layla called out in Turkish. "Put your weapon down, or they'll kill you!"

The guard hesitated only for a second then threw his rifle on to the ground and raised his arms high in the air.

The Delta Force team scattered out, looking for others who might have missed their ride out. One by one they called out from different corners of the warehouse. "Clear."

Bull rushed forward to Layla and dropped down on his knees.

"Hey, are you all right?" he asked.

She laughed. "I am now."

He pulled her into his arms. She wrapped her arms around his neck and held onto him. When he tried to bring her to her feet, she stumbled, her ankles still partially bound. He settled her back on the ground, took out his knife, and sliced through the tape, removing it from her legs.

She turned to Miriam. "Help my friend."

"I've got it," Blade called out. Blade cut the bonds off of Miriam's wrists and ankles.

Bull helped Layla to her feet.

She leaned into him, reveling, in the strength his arms provided wrapped around her.

"It was Hasan Saka," she said. "He took me to get to Miriam. He was one of the main people involved in human trafficking in the area. He wanted to take Miriam out so that he could resume operations, only I made a guess that ended up being accurate."

"And what was that?" Bull asked.

"You remember at the hotel, when the guards were firing their weapons and people were running and shouting, trying to get out?"

Bull nodded. "I remember."

"I saw Saka standing up against the wall. He made no move to leave the building. It was as if he didn't fear being shot, and he was looking to make sure the guards got who they were supposed to."

"The Minister of Justice," Bull said.

Layla nodded. "I didn't realize what he was doing then. But now, it all makes sense. He ordered the attack that killed the Minister of Justice. When I called him on it, he more or less admitted to it because he figured I wouldn't live long enough to tell anybody."

"Then he should be running scared since you've been freed." Bull's brow dipped. "And you'll be in danger of Hasan Saka targeting you again. He'll want to shut you up."

She shook her head. "I don't think so. I'm not afraid of Hasan Saka. I think he has a bigger problem. I overheard him talking on his cellphone to someone, telling him that we knew who had set up the attack on the hotel. That someone was ordering him to kill us."

"You think someone even higher up was responsible for the attack at the hotel that killed the Minister of Justice?" Rucker asked as he joined them.

Layla nodded. "The Turkish president."

Rucker whistled. "And Hasan Saka let someone go who can tell the truth and expose the president. A president who is already unpopular with the people. When they find out...if you thought that riot downtown was bad..." Rucker whistled.

Layla nodded. "Exactly."

"I don't think Hasan Saka will live through the next twenty-four hours," Bull said.

"The president will have his men take him out," Rucker said. "And now that he knows that Layla was involved, he might come after her as well."

"Which means I have to leave the country," Layla said.

"Layla, sweetheart," Bull took her hands, "you realize even if you leave the country, they can still get to you."

"I can change my name. Surely there's some kind of witness protection program I can join."

"That's not what I'm talking about. They'd still have a hold over you. One that you would not be able to ignore."

Layla's eyes narrowed. "I don't..." Her eyes widened. "My father. They could take my father hostage to get me. We have to get to my father quickly." Layla pulled free of Bull's hands and ran for the door. "We have to warn him."

Bull caught her before she reached the door of the warehouse. "Hold on. You can't just run all the way back to the embassy. I sent Dash and Dawg back for the vehicles. They should be here in a few minutes."

Layla paced as they waited in front of the warehouse for the vehicles to appear. She stopped in midstride. "I need to contact my father."

"I have his cellphone," Bull said, holding the device up. "You'd have to contact the embassy."

"Give me a phone," she demanded.

He held it out.

She snatched it from his hands, entered the number for the embassy and waited for the automated system to allow her to key in the extension for her father's office. Her father would be waiting there since they had his cellphone. She put the phone on speaker.

Her father answered on the first ring.

"Daddy," she said.

"Layla, baby, tell me you're all right?" he said, his voice strained. "I was so worried."

"I'm okay. Bull found me in time. Daddy, I'm worried about *you*. I need you to get out of the embassy and hide nearby until we can get there. I think my assistant, Pinar Erim, is a mole inside our embassy. You need to avoid her at all cost," she said. "Have you seen her this evening."

Her father answered, his tone odd, "As a matter of fact, I have. She's standing right in front of me with a gun."

CHAPTER 13

Layla's face blanched.

Bull wrapped his arm around her and pulled her close.

"Layla," her father said. "Don't come back to the embassy."

"You will come back to the embassy, or I will kill your father," Pinar said.

"Don't do it, Layla," the ambassador said.

"Daddy," Layla sobbed, "I can't leave you to those people."

"If you do not show up at the embassy in the next thirty minutes," Pinar said, "my people will burn this building to the ground with your father in it."

"No," Layla cried out. The line went dead.

Two vehicles pulled up in front of the warehouse.

"Blade, you and Dawg take Miriam," Rucker said. "Get her to where she wants to go. She needs to leave this country now. The human traffickers know who she is. She won't be safe."

Miriam nodded. "Just get me to my people. They'll take care of me."

"Lance, you go with them." The three men piled into the vehicle with Miriam and took off. Layla and Bull got into the backseat of the other vehicle, along with Mac, Dash and Tank. Rucker took the wheel.

"How long does it take to get to the embassy from here?" Layla asked.

"It took us about thirty minutes to get here," Bull said.

Her lips firmed, and she leaned over Rucker's shoulder. "Make it less."

Rucker nodded and pressed his foot to the accelerator.

Bull held one of Layla's hands with his M4A1 rifle propped between his knees.

"My father is the only family I have left," Layla whispered.

Bull squeezed her hand. "I know." He wanted to tell her that they'd get there on time. That they'd take care of her father, and that he wouldn't die. But he didn't want to make any promises he couldn't keep. "We'll do the best we can."

"Do you think Pinar is working for Hasan or the president?" Layla asked.

"How long has Pinar worked for the US embassy?"

"I'm not certain. She was there when we got there. I think that they'd said she'd been there for about six years."

"About the same amount of time that the president has been in power," Rucker commented from the front seat.

"How will we get into the embassy?" Layla said.

"You and I will walk through the front," Bull said. "They'll be expecting us. The rest of the team can come in through the hidden passageway."

Thirty minutes might as well have been a lifetime for both Bull and Layla. Each minute could be the last for Layla's father.

As they neared the embassy, Bull had Rucker drive to the back side of the compound where he pointed out the hidden doorway.

Dash, Tank and Mac jumped out, found the doorway and gave a thumbs up when they did.

Rucker drove the vehicle around to the front of the embassy and dropped Layla and Bull off at the gate.

It felt strange going through the gate like normal when Bull knew what awaited them inside.

After they passed the gate guards, Layla leaned close to Bull. "I wanted to tell them so badly that we needed help inside, but I'm not sure what Pinar will do to my father if she's cornered. And I don't know how many more of the staff inside the embassy, or on the gates, are in cahoots with her. They could have my father surrounded. Then what? We're just walking into a trap."

"But we have the team making their way inside," Bull said. "And once the others drop Miriam where she needs to go, they'll join us here at the embassy, too."

"What if Pinar knows about the tunnel? What if she has people guarding it?"

"Our guys can handle it." He tapped his headset. "Comm check," he whispered.

One by one the men on the grounds reported in.

"Any trouble in the tunnel?" he asked as they approached the embassy's front door.

"None," Dash said. "We left Tank at the entrance to guide Rucker in. Right now, Dash and I are in the library."

"Take the stairwell down to the bottom. The ambassador's office is on the first floor. We're just coming through the front entrance." Once again, Bull was without a weapon. He had left his in the vehicle with Rucker since he couldn't have gotten it past the guards at the front gate.

When they entered the foyer of the embassy, Bull put his hand in front of Layla, using his body to block hers on their way to her father's office. As they walked through the hallway, several men wearing the uniforms of the Turkish gate guards lined the hallway, each carrying a rifle. Bull counted six total. When they reached her father's office, the door was closed and a guard stood in front of it. When they approached, he opened the door and stepped back. Inside her father's office, there were no fewer than four more guards, all dressed as gate guards for the embassy.

Bull instantly sized up his opponents.

All four carried rifles, and the sheer fact that there were four of them gave him pause. He could handle two easily. Four, spread out in the room, was more of a challenge, and one that would put Layla and her father in danger of being hit with the crossfire. Not to mention that he was completely unarmed, except for the knife in his pocket.

Pinar stood beside the ambassador with a small handgun pointed at his head.

Layla tried to dart around Bull to get to her father. "Daddy."

Bull stuck his hand out and grabbed her arm to keep her from going that direction.

"Let him go," Layla demanded.

Pinar spoke to the guards in Turkish. "Tie them up."

When the guards approached Bull, he went into fight mode and threw a sidekick at the first man who reached him. He cocked his arm and hit the other one behind him with an elbow to the larynx. Before he could regroup, the other two were on him.

He fought hard, four against one. Even when they had him pinned to the ground, he twisted and bucked. His earbuds were knocked free of his ears, cutting off radio communications between him and his team. He was on his own.

Bull couldn't give up. Layla and her father depended on him. He renewed his efforts to fight free of the men holding him down.

"Keep it up, and I'll put a bullet in her head," Pinar said.

Bull looked up to find Pinar holding a gun to Layla's head. The guard with the bloody nose held both of Layla's arms behind her back. She couldn't move or duck a bullet.

Bull stopped fighting. He had to buy time. Time for his team to get to them. "Don't hurt her."

"You don't have much say in the matter, do you?" Pinar's lip curled on one corner.

"What are you going to do to us?" Layla asked.

"It's not what we're going to do, it's what the rioters are going to do." Pinar tilted her head toward the window. "As we speak, a mob is moving this way. They're under the impression that the US Ambassador orchestrated the murder of the Minister of Justice at the hotel tonight. They're angry, and they want the US out of our country."

The guards tied Bull's wrists behind his back and trussed his ankles. They did the same with Layla and her father, leaving them lying on their sides in the middle of the ambassador's office.

"Our president will be happy to know that the

rioters have served justice for the death of the minister." Pinar gave half a smile. "And don't think that your men will be able to rescue you from this. We trapped them in the library, and the escape tunnel has been closed off for good."

Pinar nodded to one of the guards.

The man left the room and returned with a five-gallon jug. He poured gasoline all around the inside walls of the office. Bull fought to break free of the rough ropes they'd used to tie his wrists. The more he tugged the tighter they seemed to get.

Pinar left the room and all the guards followed but one. The last guard struck a match and threw it into the gasoline. As the door closed behind the guard, Bull could hear the metallic sound of a key turning in the lock.

Fire erupted around the room, surrounding them in seconds, the flames consuming the fuel on the floor.

They didn't have much time to get out before the fire and smoke claimed them. But how could they get out when they were tied up?

Then Bull remembered the pocketknife in his pocket. He scooted across the floor toward Layla. "Can you reach into my pocket?"

"I don't know." Her hands were tied behind her back just like his were.

"Try," he said. "Try to get into my pocket. There's a pocketknife in there. See if you can dig it out."

She scooted her back toward him and reached as far as she could until she got both her hands into his pocket.

"I think I have it," she said.

"Can you get it open?"

"I think so," she said. Layla fumbled with the knife as the fire built and started consuming other things.

Bull counted the seconds, praying they would get out of there alive, not in body bags.

"Got it open," Layla cried.

He reached behind him, found her hands and guided the knife to the ropes around his wrists. "Saw away," he said, "And do it quickly. I don't care if you cut me, just pull hard and take it through that rope."

She sawed, working at it as best she could.

Once the flames had burned through the gasoline, they ate into the curtains by the windows. Smoke filled the air, rising up against the room's high ceilings.

The ambassador coughed. "Is there anything I can do? Please, what can I do to help?"

"I'm working on it," Layla said, tightly. "I'm getting there." She tugged and pulled.

Bull could feel the strands snap, one at a time. When the blade cut through the last strand, he pulled his hands free, rolled over, took the knife from Layla and cut through the bindings on her wrists and ankles. Then he cut through the rope around his ankles. He handed the knife to Layla. "Free your father while I work on the door, so we can get out of here."

He crawled on his hands and knees to the door to keep below the layer of smoke. As he suspected, somebody had locked it from the other side. Kicking it would do no good because it opened to the inside. He didn't have time to work the hinges loose, and he'd need a crowbar to open it otherwise. He crawled across the floor back toward the windows. He yanked down the burning curtains and stomped out the flames. The windows offered no escape. They had iron bars on the outside to keep people from breaking in. Unfortunately, it kept those trapped inside from getting out that route. If he couldn't get out from the doors or the windows, he had to find another way.

Through the window, he caught sight of a crowd moving their way, carrying flashlights, torches, rifles and machetes. They were chanting and appeared angry.

Bull's gut knotted. He had to get Layla and her father out of that room quickly. If they didn't die in the fire soon, they wouldn't be able to escape the building or the rioters heading their way. The sound of gunfire erupted in the hallway outside the door.

"Stay down!" Bull yelled to Layla and her father. Bull grabbed a rug and beat at the flames, trying to put them out so that they wouldn't die of smoke inhalation.

The gunfire ceased, and a voice called out. "Bull! Layla!"

Bull ran to the door and banged against the wooden panel. "We're in here! The door's locked. We're trapped!"

Layla had taken over with the rug, beating at the other flames. Her father did the same.

"We've got company coming." Bull yelled. "Rioters just breached the front gate."

"Stand back from the door," Rucker called out.

Bull moved away from the door. A moment later a small explosion splintered the doorframe. The door burst open, and Tank stood in the opening.

Rucker poked his head around the side. "Nothing a little C4 and Tank's sidekick couldn't handle. Come on, let's get going."

They ran to the stairwell and up to the floor where the library was.

"Pinar said that the tunnel was shut off," Bull said.

"I believe that was their intent." Rucker pushed through the stairwell door. "Someone lobbed a grenade at the exit door. Tank happened to see it, picked it up and threw it back. The tunnel remains intact. The man who threw the grenade had a bad day."

They ran up the staircase and down the hallway to the library. The door had been destroyed.

"She said she locked you guys in the library," Layla said.

Mac chuckled. "Like the ambassador's office... nothing a little C4 can't handle."

The sound of chanting and shouting was loud enough to reach their ears from down below.

"The embassy has been breached," Ambassador Grey said.

Bull nodded. "Time to go."

Rucker led the way, followed by Mac and Tank. The ambassador went next, and then Layla. Bull followed closely behind her. Dash had his back. They kept some space between them in case the tunnel was compromised. When they reached the exterior exit and stepped out into the street, a couple of vans stood waiting. Miriam Rogers poked her head out of the side door of one of them.

"Hurry up! Get in!"

"Where's the rest of my team?" Rucker asked.

The sliding door on the second van opened, and Blade leaned out and grinned. "All present and accounted for."

Bull helped Layla and her father into the van, and then got in beside them. Rucker and Mac climbed in, too. Tank and Dash dove into the second van. The driver punched the accelerator before the doors even closed.

Miriam tossed coveralls to each of them. "Put these on. You're now employees of the Atatürk Oil Company."

Bull noticed that all the people in the van wore matching coveralls.

"Since we all need a quick ride out of the country, I arranged one," Miriam said. She handed each of them a ballcap with the same logo on it as the oil company.

Layla stuffed her hair up into the cap and pulled it down low over her forehead. "How did you know to come get us?"

Miriam smiled. "I told you I have a network. I heard there was a riot headed toward the US Embassy. I figured you guys would need a way out."

Layla frowned. "How did you know where to pick us up?"

Miriam smiled. "Another informant in my network said they spotted you coming out the back way on several occasions. I assumed you'd exit the path of least resistance."

Layla's frown deepened. "You know about the secret passage into the embassy?"

Again, Miriam smiled. "I know a lot of things. And if I don't, I have people who do."

"What are you going to do?" Layla asked. "Are you leaving Turkey as well?"

Miriam drew in a deep breath and let it out. "For now. But I will be back. I'm needed here. I might wait until the current president is replaced." She shrugged. "Or sooner. In the meantime, my people will carry on."

Layla hugged the woman. "You do so much for those women, risking your life in the process."

"Mine is but one life. There are many more lives that can be saved." Miriam touched Layla's arm. "Your assistance made a difference." She turned to Rucker and Bull. "I received word that Hasan Saka's vehicle crashed on the highway, heading toward Adana. There were no survivors." Her gaze returned to Layla.

Layla shook her head. "He was a loose end the president couldn't risk unraveling."

Miriam nodded.

"Have your people keep an eye on Pinar Erim," Bull said. "She was a mole inside the US Embassy." He slipped his arm around Layla's waist. "She tried to kill Ambassador Grey and Layla."

"And you." Layla leaned into him. "And she would have succeeded, if not for your team." She shot a smile toward Rucker and Mac. "Thank you."

"We owe our lives to your team," Ambassador Grey said. "Your timing couldn't have been better." He frowned. "Anyone have a cellphone I could use? I need to report in to my contacts in Washington to let them know what's going on."

"I believe this is yours." Bull handed the ambassador his cellphone. "We couldn't have found your daughter without it."

Miriam tipped her head toward the cellphone.

"Once you're finished, turn off your phone. We don't want anyone to be able to track us."

Layla pulled her watch off. "Then I need to ditch this as well."

Miriam nodded, took the watch from Layla and handed it to the man riding in the front seat.

He rolled down the window and tossed the watch out onto the pavement.

Bull turned to Rucker. "I think it's about time to call the boss."

Rucker nodded. "Will do." He called, using his cellphone. The colonel was still in Afghanistan with another Delta Force team. He answered on the first ring. Rucker filled him in on what had happened and what they were attempting to do to get the ambassador and his daughter out of the country. Rucker listened for a few minutes and then ended the call. He turned to Miriam.

"If there's any way to get us to Incirlik, we have people who can get us the rest of the way."

She nodded. "I think we could make that happen."

The vans drove through the city, taking back roads and side streets, avoiding main thoroughfares. Eventually, they emerged into the nearby country-side not far from Ankara, turning into a gated facility with big buildings and lots of oil drilling equipment.

The guards at the gate were expecting them and let them pass through quickly. They drove around one of the sprawling buildings to the backside where a fleet of helicopters stood in a line, all with the oil company's logo.

"How many can one of those birds hold?" Layla asked.

"All of us," Miriam replied. "Are you ready to leave Turkey?"

Layla turned to her father.

He nodded. "Anything to ensure your safety."

Layla turned to Miriam, and she nodded. "We're ready."

CHAPTER 14

BULL HELPED Layla out of the van and walked with her to the waiting helicopter. He held her hand as she climbed up into the aircraft and settled into a seat, then took the one beside her.

The ambassador sat on the other side of Layla. Miriam and the rest of the Delta Force team climbed aboard.

Bull helped Layla buckle her harness, fastened his, and then took her hand. "Have you thought about what you're going to do once you leave Turkey?"

She shrugged. "I have a degree in elementary education. I could teach children."

"You know you could do that just about anywhere, don't you?" he said.

She nodded.

The pilot completed his preflight check. Once they were all inside, he started the engines.

The rotors spun, beating the air, making enough noise that they couldn't hear each other talk without speaking into the headset, but then everybody else could hear.

Bull adjusted his headset over his ears and settled in for the flight.

As they lifted into the sky, they cleared the top of the buildings and could see military vehicles headed toward the oil company compound.

"Will the oil company be in trouble for transporting us out?" Layla asked, turning toward Miriam.

"Not if they think we're transporting oil company employees. The people here will cover for us. The president gets a kickback on sales. He won't do anything to harm them." Miriam looked to Rucker and Bull. "To the airbase at Incirlik?"

Rucker nodded.

She passed the information to the pilot in Turkish. "The pilot will give the air traffic controller a final destination that fits one of their drilling sites south of Adana. The pilot can request a refueling stop at the Adana airport. I'll have my network set up some transportation from that airport to Incirlik."

Before they got too far away from Ankara, Miriam texted on her phone, her thumbs flying over the keys. A few minutes later she looked up. "We're all set. You might as well sit back and relax. It'll be a little less than two hours before we get there."

Layla leaned her head on Bull's shoulder and held

his hand throughout the flight. She nodded off after they had only been thirty minutes in the air.

The fact that Layla and her father had to leave Turkey opened up an entirely new world of possibilities in Bull's mind. Layla's degree in elementary education meant she could go to work practically anywhere Stateside. Even near posts where he could be stationed.

Was it possible, as Rucker had said, to have a relationship with somebody and still remain Delta Force?

Or would Layla continue to follow her father in whatever endeavors he chose next? There was only one way to find out, and that was to ask her. No matter which direction Layla went, Bull was destined to go back to Afghanistan and rejoin the rest of his unit.

They weren't due to redeploy to the States any time soon that he knew of. Dating virtually wouldn't be the same as dating in person. It wouldn't be fair to tell Layla to wait for him to get back.

And he was back to his original conclusion that being a Delta did not bode well for relationships.

He must have nodded off somewhere between Ankara and Adana. When he opened his eyes again, the motion of the rotor blades had changed as they hovered over a landing pad on the general aviation side of the Adana International airport. The pad was situated outside a hangar with the Atatürk Oil

Company logo emblazoned in large red letters on the front.

It was still dark outside as the chopper kissed the ground, settling onto the tarmac. The sun would rise soon on their last day in Turkey. Hopefully, Ambassador Grey and his daughter would be on their way to the States before then.

They waited for the blades to stop spinning before disembarking.

Two dark vans appeared and pulled up beside the chopper.

"Bull, Dash, Blade, stay here," Rucker said. "Let us go first."

With their weapons drawn, Rucker, Mac, Tank and Dawg climbed out of the chopper.

"I'm coming, too," Miriam said and dropped to the tarmac. "They're expecting me."

Once they gave a thumbs-up, Tank and Blade helped the ambassador down.

Bull climbed out and lifted Layla to the ground, holding onto her waist a little longer than necessary. He wanted to say something, but they didn't really have the time. Instead, he pressed a brief kiss to her forehead, took her hand and walked with her to the waiting vans.

Once they were all inside, they pulled away from the hangar. Another vehicle pulled in front of them as they drove out onto the street and still another fell in behind them.

The vans took off, driving through the streets of Adana to the US military base in Incirlik. When they reached the gate, a full bird colonel approached the vans. He leaned his head into the first vehicle's driver's side and asked. "Is one of you Ambassador Grey?"

The ambassador responded. "That would be me."

The colonel popped to attention and saluted. "Sir, welcome to Incirlik. Though your stay will be short, it's an honor. Let me know if there's anything we can do to make you more comfortable."

"Thank you, Colonel," Ambassador Grey said.

Layla squeezed Bull's hand. "You don't know how relieved it makes me feel to hear another American welcoming us to an American military base."

Bull nodded. He felt the same. "Don't count your chickens yet. You're not out of Turkey."

She squeezed his hand again. "I know."

The vans took them directly to a flight line where a C-130 Hercules airplane stood waiting for them.

As they climbed out of the vans, Rucker pulled Bull aside. "You know we're not going where they're going."

Bull sighed. "I know." He'd expected as much. His duty was to the US Army. "I'd like to see them up into the plane and settled before we go our way."

Rucker nodded. "We'll be in the terminal. Our plane hasn't arrived yet." Rucker gave him a stern look. "Don't be on that plane when it takes off."

Bull smiled. "I won't." He still had a job to do, and if it wasn't in Turkey, it was back in Afghanistan.

Rucker's expression softened. "Give her your number so you can keep in touch."

The colonel led Ambassador Grey into the plane and found him a seat.

Bull walked with Layla into the plane and sat in the seat beside her. He wanted to hold her hand one last time before she left, if only for a few minutes before they closed the doors.

"I guess this is where we say goodbye," he said. He lifted her hand and kissed the backs of her knuckles.

She stared at her knuckles with a tremulous smile. "Thank you for getting me here safely," she said, "and for getting my father out of the embassy."

"It was my pleasure." God, he sounded so formal when he was feeling anything but formal.

She looked up into his eyes. "Where are you headed from here?"

"Probably back to my team in the sandbox."

She nodded, her eyes welling with tears. "Will I see you again?"

Her tears tore at his heart. "I told you it wasn't a good idea to get involved with a Delta."

"Yeah, and when have I ever listened to you?" She smiled as those tears slipped down her cheeks. Layla cupped his cheeks and pulled him down to kiss her.

Time was running out, and there were so many things he wanted to say. He pulled the note she had written out of his pocket and unfolded it in front of her. "Did you mean what you wrote?"

She shook her head. "No, well, not anymore anyway." She drew in a breath and let it out.

Bull nodded. "I understand. You're probably ready for me to go." He started to get up.

"Wait," she said, "I don't mean what I wrote then, now."

He frowned. "I'm not sure what you mean?"

She pointed at the note. "On the note, I said I think I love you. I don't think I love you anymore."

"Yeah, that really hurts." He pressed a hand to his chest, his heart breaking. "But I do understand. I want you to know, even though I love you and though there's no future in our relationship, you'll always be in my heart." He lifted her hand and pressed her palm to his cheek.

"You love me?" she asked.

He gave her a crooked smile. "I swore I'd never let it happen, but then you became my assignment..." He smiled sadly. "I couldn't help myself."

Her brow twisted. "Even though we've only known each other for a couple of days?"

He grinned. "I guess when you know, you know. But don't worry, if you don't feel the same way, that's okay. I'll survive."

She laughed.

He frowned. "It's not funny." He touched his chest. "I'm really hurting."

She took the note from him, leaned over her chair and summoned the flight attendant. "Do you have a pen?"

The flight attendant handed her one.

Layla took the pen then scratched through the word "think" and handed the note back to him. "You don't get it," she said, "I don't *think* I love you anymore. I *know*."

Bull's breaking heart filled with joy.

The flight attendant chose that moment to say, "Sir, you'll have to deplane. We're about to take off."

Bull tore a strip of paper off the bottom of Layla's note, took the pen from Layla and scribbled his phone number on it. He handed the paper to her as he stood. "When you get a new phone, call me. I'd like to keep in touch."

Her eyebrows lifted. "You mean as in having a relationship?"

He nodded. "I'm game if you are."

She smiled. "I'm always up for an adventure. Especially with someone I love."

"Oh, sweetheart. Those three words are music to my ears. I love you, too." He bent and pressed a kiss to her lips. "Oh, and my real name is Craig Bullington, not Greg Smith. That's why they call me Bull. Short for Bullington. Greg Smith was my cover for working in the embassy."

Her brows rose. "Do I even know you?"

He touched his chest. "You know what counts.

Names are just names." He kissed her again. "I'll let you know when I'm back in the States." He turned and hurried toward the exit.

"I'll be there waiting to welcome you home," she called out after him.

EPILOGUE

Two months later

As his flight landed at the small airport in Temple, Texas, Bull peered out the airplane window at the terminal, as if he might see someone familiar standing in one of the floor-to-ceiling windows. He knew it wasn't possible when he'd have to get to the baggage claim area first. He unbuckled his seatbelt before the aircraft came to a full stop. They had to wait for the jet bridge to be rolled up to the fuselage.

Rucker leaned around Bull, who had the window seat. "Can't wait to get off this plane and hold Nora in my arms."

"Is she meeting you here?" Bull asked.

"Damn right. It's been too long."

"What about you, Dash?" Bull asked. "Is Sunny going to be here?"

"No way," he said. "I told her I wanted her all to myself, not with a mob of paparazzi all around her. She'll be at our apartment, waiting for me to get there. Alone."

"What about Layla? Does she know you're coming?" Rucker asked.

"I gave her the flight information. She wasn't sure she could get off work in the middle of the day to be here. It depends on whether or not she got a sub to fill in."

"Sounds to me like she's settling into the Ft. Hood, Texas, area." Rucker grinned. "You two going to make it real?"

"Real?"

Rucker punched his shoulder. "Your engagement, dumbass."

"We'll see."

"Another one bites it." Blade shook his head.

"Just wait, Blade," Dash said. "You'll be next."

"Nope. I'm a confirmed bachelor." Blade laced his fingers behind his neck and stretched. "No one woman is worth giving up all of them."

"You're an ass," Dash said. "I'm betting you'll fall the hardest of all of us within the next year."

"Want to put money on that?" Blade stuck out his hand. "Fifty bucks says I don't."

"Make it a hundred." Dash shook hands with Blade.

They'd caught a military flight from Afghanistan to Germany. After a forty-eight-hour layover, they'd boarded a commercial flight for home.

The layover had given Bull the opportunity to do a little shopping. Over the past two months, he and Layla had kept in touch with video conferences, calls and text messages when they'd had internet connection in the field.

They'd even exchanged letters. Hers always managed to get to him about three weeks after she'd sent them. He'd probably get some forwarded back to his apartment in Temple. He'd kept every one of the letters along with the note that she had written that said *I love you*.

Layla's father had taken a position at the Pentagon and settled into a townhouse in Virginia.

Layla had chosen to take a teaching job near Fort Hood where Bull was stationed. He'd taken it as a sign she was willing to move their relationship to the next level. He hoped he was right.

Bull's leg bounced as he waited impatiently for the flight attendant to open the door. When she did, he was out of his seat and down the aisles, anxious to get to baggage claim and Layla.

It would be a while before they made it that far. They still had to wait in the long lines to go through customs. Once they emerged in the baggage claim area, he craned his neck looking for her.

"Can you see Nora?" Rucker pushed past him.

"Not yet," Bull said, but he wasn't looking for Nora. He was looking for a dark-haired beauty who had promised to meet him at the airport if she could.

Then he saw her, and his heart swelled with happiness.

Layla stood near their baggage carousel holding a sign high above her head. The sign had huge letters in gold glitter that spelled out, I LOVE YOU. When she spotted him, she grinned and waved the sign higher.

Then she pulled another sign from behind it.

IF YOU'RE ASKING...

Bull's brow wrinkled.

She dropped that sign to reveal the next one, also in bright gold glitter.

I'M SAYING YES!

Bull laughed and ran to her. He crushed her in his arms for a brief moment, then set her on her feet and dropped to one knee. He held up the box he'd picked up in Germany and opened it to display the diamond ring inside.

"I love you, Layla Grey." He laughed. "And I'm asking."

Her eyes filled with tears, and she dropped to her knees in front of him. "And I'm saying yes."

Bull slipped the ring onto her finger. He couldn't

believe he'd found the woman of his dreams. And she'd agreed to marry him.

Rucker, with Nora in the curve of his arms, leaned close to Bull. "Who said relationships don't work when you're a Delta?"

Nora elbowed Rucker in the side. "Shut up and let them kiss."

Bull pulled Layla into his arms and sealed their love with a kiss.

SEAL SALVATION

BROTHERHOOD PROTECTORS COLORADO
BOOK #1

New York Times & *USA Today*
Bestselling Author

ELLE JAMES

New York Times & USA Today Bestselling Author

ELLE JAMES

CHAPTER 1

JAKE COGBURN SAT in the tattered lounge chair he'd scavenged on the side of the street after moving into an empty apartment in Colorado Springs. He hadn't planned on living in an apartment, nor had he planned on sleeping on the only piece of furniture he could afford without digging into his savings. He'd put aside money to purchase a plot of land out in the middle of nowhere Colorado. On that land, he'd wanted to build a house.

All those plans had been blown away, along with the lower half of his left leg, when he'd stepped on an IED in Afghanistan. Yeah, he had the money in the bank, but what good did it do him? On one leg, what could he accomplish? Working a piece of land and building a house took all four limbs.

He poured another tumbler of whiskey and tipped the contents up, letting the cool liquid burn a path down his throat. Soon, the numbing effect set in. Jake could almost forget the phantom pain in his missing leg, could almost forget he'd not only lost a leg, but had lost the only family he'd ever had.

As a Navy SEAL, his teammates had been his brothers. Every one of them would lay down his life for him, as he'd taken one for the team when his foot had landed on that IED.

Medically discharged, having gone through multiple surgeries and physical therapy, he'd been dumped out into a civilian world that had no use for a one-legged, former Navy SEAL.

What was he good for? His skillset included demolitions, tactical operations, highly effective weapons firing and hand-to-hand combat.

Where could he find that kind of work in a civilian occupation? And doing all that balanced on one leg?

Nope.

He was all washed up. His only hope was to sit on a corner with his hat held out, begging like a hundred other homeless veterans roaming the streets of Colorado Springs.

His free hand clenched into a fist. Jake had never begged for anything in his life. He'd fought for what he'd accomplished. From surviving the gangs on the streets of Denver, to forging his way through BUD/S training, he'd always counted on his mind and brute strength to get through any hardship.

But now…

Through the empty glass tumbler, he stared down at the stump below his left knee then slammed the glass against the wall. It hit hard and shattered into a million pieces that scattered across the floor.

A knock sounded on the door to his apartment.

"I didn't put a dent in the damned wall!" he yelled. "Leave me the fuck alone."

"Jake Cogburn?" An unfamiliar male voice called out from the other side of the faded wooden panel.

"Yeah," Jake muttered. "I'm not interested in buying anything."

"I'm not selling anything," the muffled voice sounded.

"Then get the fuck away from my door," Jake said and tipped the bottle of whiskey up, downing the last swallow. The bottle followed the glass, hitting the wall with a solid thump before it crashed to the wooden floor and bounced.

"Everything all right in there?" the man called out.

"Who the hell cares?" Jake muttered.

"I do."

Jake frowned. "I told you. I'm not buying anything."

"And I told you I'm not selling anything." A moment of silence followed. "Would you open the door for a brother?"

Anger surged through Jake. "I don't have a brother. I'm an only fuckin' child."

"Then how about a brother-in-arms? A fellow spec ops guy? A Delta Force man?"

Jake barked a single laugh. "Yeah. Yeah. Whatever. The SEALs don't operate out of Colorado. And as far as I know, there isn't a Delta Force unit near here."

"Not active Delta Force," the man fired back. "Look. A friend sent me to offer you a job."

"I don't have any friends," Jake said, then added muttering beneath his breath, "and I'm not fit for any jobs."

"You're fit for the job he's got in mind," the man said. "Look, Cog, the only easy day was yesterday. Are you a SEAL or not?"

Cog.

Only the men he'd fought with side by side had called him Cog.

A frown pulled his brow low as he leaned forward in his chair. "Anyone can look up the SEAL motto. How do I know you're the real deal?" Jake had to admit he was curious now.

"You have to trust me." The man chuckled. "It's not like us Deltas have tridents tattooed on our foreheads like you Navy SEALs. My honor was forged in battle, just like yours."

Despite himself, Jake's lips twitched. No, they didn't have tridents, the symbol of their trade, drawn in indelible ink on their foreheads. But it was etched into their hearts. The grueling training they'd survived had made them proud to wear the symbol of the Navy SEAL and even prouder to fight as a team alongside the Delta Force operatives.

"Who sent you?" Jake asked.

"Hank Patterson," the voice said and waited.

A flood of memories washed over Jake. Hank had been his mentor when he'd come on board, fresh from BUD/S training. He hadn't hazed him as the others on the team had. He'd taken Jake beneath his wing and taught him everything he knew that would help him in the many missions to come. Many of Hank's techniques had kept Jake alive on more than one occasion. He owed the man his life.

"Why didn't Hank come himself?" Jake asked.

"He and his wife have a new baby. You might not be aware that his wife is a famous actress. She's going on set in a few days, and Hank has diaper duty."

"Hank? Diaper duty?" Jake shook his head. The alcohol in his system made his vision blur. "Doesn't sound like Hank."

"Well, it is. Will you open the door so we can discuss his proposition?"

Jake glanced around the pathetic excuse of an apartment and shook his head. "No. But I'll come out in a minute. You can buy me a drink, and we can talk."

"Good," the man said. "Anything to get out of this hallway. Your neighbors are giving me threatening looks."

Jake reached for his prosthesis, pulled up his

pantleg, donned the inner sleeve, slipped his stump into position and pulled the outer sleeve over his thigh. He slid his good foot into a shoe and pushed to a standing position, swaying slightly.

He smelled like dirty clothes and alcohol. But he'd be damned if he let Hank's emissary into the apartment to see how low Jake Cogburn had sunk.

Lifting his shirt up to his nose, he grimaced. Then he yanked it over his head, slung it across the room and reached into the duffel bag in the corner for another T-shirt.

The sniff test had him flinging that shirt across the room to land with the other in a heap on the floor. Two shirts later, he settled on a black Led Zeppelin T-shirt that had been a gift from one of his buddies on his last SEAL team. The man had been a fan of one of the biggest bands of the seventies, a time way before he'd been born.

Running a hand through his hair, he shoved his socked-foot and his prosthetic foot into a pair of boots and finally opened the door.

The man on the other side leaned against the opposite wall in the hallway. He pushed away from the wall and held out his hand. "Jake Cogburn, I'm Joseph Kuntz. My friends call me Kujo."

Jake gave the man a narrow-eyed glare but took the hand. "What kind of job does Hank have in mind. Not that I'm interested." He shook the hand and let go quickly.

"He's started a business up in Montana and wants to open up a branch here in Colorado." Kujo ran his glance over Jake.

Jake's shoulders automatically squared. "And?"

"And he wants you to head it up."

Jake laughed out loud. "Hank wants this broken-down SEAL to head up an office?"

Kujo nodded. "He does."

"Why don't *you* do it?"

"I have a pregnant wife back in Montana. I only have a few weeks to help you lay the groundwork. Then I have to get back."

His head shaking back and forth, Jake stared at the man as if he'd lost his mind. "What the hell kind of business can a one-legged ex-SEAL manage? Does he even know me?"

"He said he mentored you as a newbie SEAL a long time back. He knows your service record and thinks you would make the perfect man to lead the new branch." Kujo crossed his arms over his chest. "He has confidence that you have the skills needed to do the job. And there's no such thing as an ex-SEAL. Once a SEAL, always a SEAL. "

Jake nodded. The man was right. "He knew me back then. But does he know me now?" Jake touched the thigh of his injured leg.

Kujo nodded. "He knows about your circumstances, and he's still certain you're the one to do the job."

Jake shook his head. "What exactly will this branch of his business sell?"

"We're a service organization. We provide security and unique skills to our clients to protect them and/or take care of situations law enforcement or the military might not be in a position to assist with."

"Vigilantes?" Kujo held up his hands. "No thanks."

"Not vigilantes," Kujo said. "More a security service for those in need of highly trained special ops folks who know how to handle a gun and run a tactical mission."

"Again," Jake said, "sounds like vigilantes. No thanks. Besides, I'm not fit to fight. The Navy told me so." He turned to go back into his apartment and find another whiskey glass.

Kujo stepped between him and the door. "Can you fire a weapon?"

Jake shrugged. "Sure. Nothing wrong with my hands and arms. But I can't run, jump and maneuver the way I used to before…" He tipped his chin toward his prosthesis.

"You still have a brain. You can compensate," Kujo raised his eyebrows. "Do you have a job?"

Jake's chest tightened. "No."

Kujo's chin lifted a fraction. "Then, what do you have to lose?" He stood with his shoulders back, his head held high—the way Jake used to stand.

What did he have to lose? He'd lost everything that had been important to him. He couldn't sink any lower. His brows furrowing, he stared into Kujo's open, friendly face and then shrugged. "I have nothing to lose."

Kujo nodded. "Trust me. I've been there. Hank Patterson brought me out of the hell I'd sunk into. Life has only gotten better since."

"Well, you have both legs," Jake pointed out.

"And you have your hands and mind, one perfectly good leg and a prosthetic device you can get around on just fine from what I can see." He frowned. "Are you going to stand around bellyaching or come with me and start a new job I think you'll love."

"I'm not bellyaching," Jake grumbled.

"But you're wasting daylight, and I have another place I need to be before dark." Kujo stood back. "What's it to be?"

For a tense moment, Jake stood fast. After weeks of wallowing in the hovel of an apartment, getting out seemed more difficult than staying with the familiar.

"Why did Hank choose me?" he asked.

"Based on your past performance as a Navy SEAL, Hank thought you were the right person for the task he had in mind. He trusts you, your work and your integrity. The job won't always be easy..." Kujo grinned. "But the only easy day..."

"Yeah, yeah...was yesterday." Jake impatiently waved Kujo ahead of him. "I'm coming. But don't take that as a yes. I have yet to decide whether I want to work for Hank."

Kujo cocked an eyebrow. "You have a better job offer?"

Jake wanted to tell the man that he did, but he couldn't. "No."

"Fine. Come with me. We have another stop to make before we seal this deal and kick off this project." Kujo nodded toward the interior of the apartment. "Got a go bag?"

Jake glanced back. "Not since I left the service. Why?"

"We'll most likely stay the night where we're going. Maybe longer. Grab what you need for a couple of days."

Jake returned to his apartment, grabbed the duffel bag out of the bottom of the closet and stuffed a pair of jeans, socks, underwear, some T-shirts, a jacket and his shaving kit into it. He returned to his apartment entrance where Kujo waited.

The other man stepped outside and waited for Jake to follow.

Jake carried his bag through the door and pulled it closed behind him. "Where are we going?"

"To a ranch."

His feet coming to an immediate halt, Jake shook his head. "Why are we going to a ranch? You didn't say anything about a ranch."

Kujo drew in a deep breath and let it go slowly, as

if he was holding back his own impatience. "Bear with me. I'll fill you in when we get there. Just suffice it to say, your job will be important to someone."

"Who?"

Kujo grinned. "Whoever needs you most."

"That's kind of vague, if you ask me."

"It's the nature of the work," Kujo said.

"Just what exactly does this job entail?" Jake asked.

"Don't worry." Kujo led the way down the stairs of the apartment complex and out to a shiny, black SUV. "I fully intend to brief you on your position and the nature of Hank's organization. But first, I'd like to get out of here and up into the mountains."

Jake climbed into the SUV, silently cursing his prosthetic when it banged against the door. Once in his seat, he buckled his seatbelt, wondering what the hell he was doing and when the hell he'd get that drink Kujo promised. Thankfully, he hadn't committed to anything, which was his only saving grace. What kind of job could Hank have in mind for a one-legged, former Navy SEAL?

ABOUT THE AUTHOR

ELLE JAMES also writing as MYLA JACKSON is a *New York Times* and *USA Today* Bestselling author of books including cowboys, intrigues and paranormal adventures that keep her readers on the edges of their seats. When she's not at her computer, she's traveling, snow skiing, boating, or riding her ATV, dreaming up new stories. Learn more about Elle James at www.ellejames.com

Website | Facebook | Twitter | GoodReads | Newsletter | BookBub | Amazon

Or visit her alter ego Myla Jackson at
mylajackson.com
Website | Facebook | Twitter | Newsletter

Follow Me!
www.ellejames.com
ellejames@ellejames.com

Montana Dog Soldier (#6)

Montana SEAL Daddy (#7)

Montana Ranger's Wedding Vow (#8)

Montana SEAL Undercover Daddy (#9)

Cape Cod SEAL Rescue (#10)

Montana SEAL Friendly Fire (#11)

Montana SEAL's Mail-Order Bride (#12)

SEAL Justice (#13)

Ranger Creed (#14)

Delta Force Rescue (#15)

Montana Rescue (Sleeper SEAL)

Hot SEAL Salty Dog (SEALs in Paradise)

Hot SEAL Bachelor Party (SEALs in Paradise)

Hot SEAL, Independence Day (SEALs in Paradise)

Brotherhood Protectors Vol 1

The Outrider Series

Homicide at Whiskey Gulch (#1)

Hideout at Whiskey Gulch (#2)

Hellfire Series

Hellfire, Texas (#1)

Justice Burning (#2)

Smoldering Desire (#3)

Hellfire in High Heels (#4)

Playing With Fire (#5)

Up in Flames (#6)

Total Meltdown (#7)

Take No Prisoners Series

SEAL's Honor (#1)

SEAL'S Desire (#2)

SEAL's Embrace (#3)

SEAL's Obsession (#4)

SEAL's Proposal (#5)

SEAL's Seduction (#6)

SEAL'S Defiance (#7)

SEAL's Deception (#8)

SEAL's Deliverance (#9)

SEAL's Ultimate Challenge (#10)

Billionaire Online Dating Service

The Billionaire Husband Test (#1)

The Billionaire Cinderella Test (#2)

The Billionaire Bride Test (#3)

The Billionaire Daddy Test (#4)

The Billionaire Matchmaker Test (#5)

The Billionaire Glitch Date (#6)

The Billionaire Perfect Date (#7) coming soon

The Billionaire Replacement Date (#8) coming soon

The Billionaire Wedding Date (#9) coming soon

Hearts & Heroes Series

Wyatt's War (#1)

Mack's Witness (#2)

Ronin's Return (#3)

Sam's Surrender (#4)

Cajun Magic Mystery Series

Voodoo on the Bayou (#1)

Voodoo for Two (#2)

Deja Voodoo (#3)

Cajun Magic Mysteries Books 1-3

Texas Billionaire Club

Tarzan & Janine (#1)

Something To Talk About (#2)

Who's Your Daddy (#3)

Love & War (#4)

Declan's Defenders

Marine Force Recon (#1)

Show of Force (#2)

Full Force (#3)

Driving Force (#4)

Tactical Force (#5)

Disruptive Force (#6)

Mission: Six

One Intrepid SEAL

Two Dauntless Hearts

Three Courageous Words

Four Relentless Days

Five Ways to Surrender

Six Minutes to Midnight

Ballistic Cowboy

Hot Combat (#1)

Hot Target (#2)

Hot Zone (#3)

Hot Velocity (#4)

SEAL Of My Own

Navy SEAL Survival

Navy SEAL Captive

Navy SEAL To Die For

Navy SEAL Six Pack

Devil's Shroud Series

Deadly Reckoning (#1)

Deadly Engagement (#2)

Deadly Liaisons (#3)

Deadly Allure (#4)

Deadly Obsession (#5)

Deadly Fall (#6)

Thunder Horse Series

Hostage to Thunder Horse (#1)

Thunder Horse Heritage (#2)

Thunder Horse Redemption (#3)

Christmas at Thunder Horse Ranch (#4)

Demon Series

Hot Demon Nights (#1)

Demon's Embrace (#2)

Tempting the Demon (#3)

Lords of the Underworld

Witch's Initiation (#1)

Witch's Seduction (#2)

The Witch's Desire (#3)

Possessing the Witch (#4)

Stealth Operations Specialists (SOS)

Nick of Time

Alaskan Fantasy

Boys Behaving Badly Anthology

Rogues (#1)

Blue Collar (#2)

Pirates (#3)

Stranded (#4)

First Responder (#5)

Blown Away

Warrior's Conquest

Enslaved by the Viking Short Story

Conquests

Smokin' Hot Firemen

Protecting the Colton Bride

Protecting the Colton Bride & Colton's Cowboy Code

Heir to Murder

Secret Service Rescue

High Octane Heroes

Haunted

Engaged with the Boss

Cowboy Brigade

Time Raiders: The Whisper

Bundle of Trouble

Killer Body

Operation XOXO

An Unexpected Clue

Baby Bling

Made in the USA
Middletown, DE
11 January 2023

21804897R00126